A MIGHTY **MARVEL** CHAPTER BOOK

SPECTACULAR ADVENTURES!

3 Books in 1

marvelkids.com

First Paperback Edition, October 2016 10 9 8 7 6 5 4 3 2 1
Library of Congress Control Number on file
FAC-029261-16232
ISBN 978-1-4847-6732-0

Star-Lord: Knowhere to Run originally published in 2014, and *Falcon: Fight or Flight* and *Ant-Man: Zombie Repellent* originally published in 2015 by Marvel Press, an imprint of Disney Book Group.

SUSTAINABLE
FORESTRY
INITIATIVE

Certified Sourcing

www.sfiprogram.org
SFI-01415

FIGHT or FLIGHT

KNOWHERE TO RUN

ZOMBIE REPELLENT

Los Angeles
New York

FIGHT OR FLIGHT

STARRING

FALCON

BY **CHRIS "DOC" WYATT**

ILLUSTRATED BY

TOM GRUMMETT, DREW GERACI,
AND **ANDY TROY**

FEATURING YOUR FAVORITES!

FALCON

SAM WILSON

CAPTAIN AMERICA

IRON MAN

HULK

THOR

HAWKEYE

BLACK WIDOW

QUICKSILVER

SCARLET WITCH

VISION

ULTRON

OUTRIDERS

TACOS

TONY STARK

ICE CREAM

THE STORY OF FALCON

*T*here came a day unlike any other, when Earth's Mightiest Heroes were united against a common threat. On that day, the Avengers were born, and **SAM WILSON** was their biggest fan. While still in school, Sam followed every one of the Avengers' battles by watching them on TV and reading about them online.

Sam dreamed that one day he, too, could be

an Avenger. . . . But how could he? He wasn't a great hero, and he didn't have super powers. However, Sam was extremely smart, and he knew how to work hard. He excelled at his studies, and he spent all his spare time inventing new machines.

While still just a teenager, Sam Wilson found himself trapped with Captain America on a tropical island run by the villainous **RED SKULL**. After a long battle, the two escaped, but barely. Cap was so impressed with Sam's skills, he suggested Sam train with him. Sam was accepted to the **S.H.I.E.L.D.** training program, and the two trained together and soon became best friends.

During his time at **S.H.I.E.L.D.**, Sam created an amazing invention—a personal wing-suit that gave him the power of flight at high speed. Wearing that suit on dangerous missions earned Sam the code name FALCON.

One day, after an adventure as Falcon, Sam came back to headquarters to find **TONY STARK**, the Avenger known as **IRON MAN**, waiting for him. Tony explained that the AVENGERS were adding a few new members to their team. . . . Would Sam be interested in joining?

Join the team that he'd loved since he was a boy? Become an Avenger, one of Earth's Mightiest Heroes? Oh, yeah, Sam was definitely interested. In fact, it was the best day of his life!

CHAPTER

1

A gentle breeze rippled through the forest of tall, majestic redwoods. From where he sat positioned in the crook of a thick branch at the top of one of the trees, **Sam Wilson**, the Avenger known as **Falcon**, could see the forest all around him. It was a fantastic view, but he wasn't really enjoying it, because there was only one thing he was interested in. . . .

Using the heads-up display in his costume's visor, Sam zoomed his vision in on something in one of the other trees. Someone just casually walking through the forest would never have spotted it, it was so well camouflaged—but Sam could see it.

It was a small wooden platform, built into the tree limbs, behind some branches. On that platform was the one thing that Falcon most wanted in the world right then. . . **a small Blue flag**.

Falcon scanned the area. There was no sign of his opponent. No sound, either. He smiled to himself. Finally, after all this time, success was going to be his.

Sam whispered into the Avengers **"comm,"** or communications unit, in his ear, signaling two **S.H.I.E.L.D.** agents who were assigned to his team. "Okay," said Falcon. "It's go time. Converge on the target in **three . . . two . . . one . . . NOW!"**

Falcon suddenly leapt out from
his tree, spreading out his wings,
which let him fly across the forest toward
his target. At the same time, the two

S.H.I.E.L.D. agents leapt from their hiding places on the ground. All three figures moved quickly, but fastest of all was Falcon. Hours and hours of practice with the wing-suit gave him surprising speed and maneuverability.

Within seconds, Falcon could see the flag almost in front of him. All he had to do was reach out and . . .

BAM!

Falcon got slammed in the side so suddenly that it knocked the breath out of him! Someone had jumped out of a hiding place and tackled him in midair.

But it wasn't just "someone." It was none other than **Captain America**! Falcon tried to push Cap off him, but Cap held firm! With all the added weight, Falcon dropped out of the sky! He and Cap were still grappling when they landed in a barrel roll on the ground.

"Fancy running into you here," joked Cap as he sprang back to his feet and hurled his famous shield. Cap's shield bounced around the forest, ricocheting off of some trees, before first taking down one **S.H.I.E.L.D.** agent, then the other. Falcon barely had time to rise to his feet before Cap had him covered again. Cap's shield landed effortlessly back in his hands.

"Well, Sam, what do you say?" asked Cap, a smile on his face.

"Yeah, you win, Cap," Falcon admitted, his shoulders drooping.

"Don't feel bad," Cap said, throwing an arm around his friend. "No one's ever beaten me in a 'capture the flag' training exercise."

"I'll be the first," admitted Sam. "Jarvis, end the program."

"Yes, sir," came a disembodied computer voice out of the sky as the whole forest—the trees, the ground, even the two **S.H.I.E.L.D.** agents—suddenly shimmered and then disappeared. All that could be seen now were the drab walls of the Avengers Tower's training room.

The whole thing had been a simulation, run by Jarvis, the Avengers Tower's computer system!

Cap and Falcon walked through a now-visible door and out into the hallway, as Cap said to

Falcon, "You're really coming along. You got very close, and also, having the two simulated **S.H.I.E.L.D.** agents on your team makes it a leadership exercise, so——"

Falcon didn't get to hear the end of Cap's thought, because Iron Man interrupted, racing down the hallway toward them. "Cap! Sam!" Iron Man shouted urgently. "Come with me right now. It's an EMERGENCY!"

"What is it now?" asked Sam. "Did Thor and Hulk get into another fight over who ate the last pint of ice cream?"

"Worse, much worse," Iron Man said gravely. "Hurry and see!"

Cap and Sam didn't miss another beat. They took off running after Iron Man.

CHAPTER 2

Sam and Cap raced after Iron Man, following him into his lab. It was a place Sam knew well, having spent hundreds of hours working there on various inventions. His talent for dreaming up new technology was one of the reasons that Sam had wanted to become an Avenger.

One day, when Sam had been aboard the **S.H.I.E.L.D.** Helicarrier when Tony Stark, the man inside the Iron Man armor, had walked right up to him.

"They tell me your name is Sam," Tony had said. **"I want to talk to you about those wings of yours."**

Stark had been so impressed with the wing-pack, as well as Sam's other inventions,

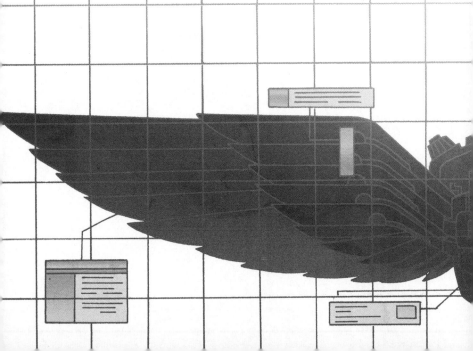

that he had invited Sam to come meet with the other Avengers.

Now Sam was eager to find out what this emergency was. If it had the usually unflappable Iron Man this upset, then it must be something serious, Sam thought.

"What happened?" asked Hulk, who was already standing in the lab with Thor when Cap, Iron Man, and Sam arrived.

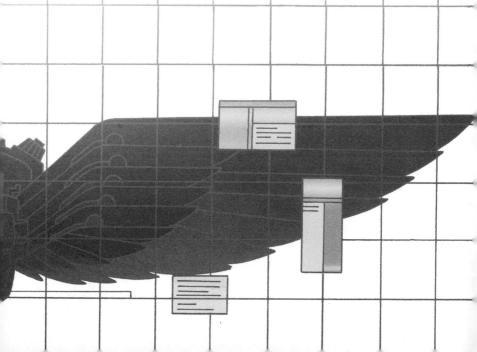

"Yes, Stark, why the alarm?" asked Thor.
"I was about to beat Hulk at a game of truck tossing."

"Beat HULK? Dream on, blondie," sneered Hulk.

"An alarm came from one of my deep-space probes that . . ." Iron Man started, then trailed off. "Wait. Did you say 'truck tossing'? Where did you get the trucks? You haven't been down in the

Stark Industries garage again, have you?"

Hulk and Thor quickly looked down, avoiding Iron Man's glare. "Well...the thing is..." said Thor, sounding guilty.

"Focus," Cap interrupted. "Tony, what's this emergency?"

Iron Man remembered why they were all there. **"The probe picked up interstellar chatter indicating that...Thanos is back."**

The air in the room was heavy. THANOS was an intergalactic alien warlord of incredible strength whom the team had tangled with before. The last time they had met Thanos, the Avengers had saved Earth from his plans for its destruction...but only barely. If Thanos came back with an army...well, it was unthinkable!

"According to the chatter, THANOS is amassing an army of Outriders just outside the orbit of Pluto. Once his invasion fleet is fully assembled, he intends to attack!" continued Iron Man. "We have to go check this trouble out . . .

NOW!"

Iron Man pointed to Cap, Hulk, and Thor as he said, **"It should be the four of us to go. Sam can stay here and mind the fort with the others."**

The whole team agreed.

A few minutes later, Sam watched as Iron Man, Cap, Hulk, and Thor loaded into one of the *QUINJETS* and prepared for launch into space.

"What do I do while you're gone?" Sam asked Cap as he headed up the ship's ramp.

"You do what you think is best. The others will look to you for leadership," Cap said, referring to the members of the Avengers who weren't going on the space mission. **"With us gone, you're in charge, Sam,"** Cap concluded as the ship's door shut between them.

In charge ... Sam thought as he watched the Quinjet disappear into the atmosphere, bound for outer space.

I'M IN CHARGE... OF THE AVENGERS!

CHAPTER 3

*A*fter Iron Man, Cap, Hulk, and Thor's ship disappeared into the sky, the first thing Sam did was send a message to the other Avengers, asking them to meet. Within minutes he walked into the Avengers Tower's briefing room to find them already waiting for him.

"Thanks for coming, every-body," said Sam as he went to the head of the table. Looking around, he was proud to be on a team with each of these heroes.

There was **Natasha Romanoff**, the **Black Widow**, a **S.H.I.E.L.D.** master spy and specialist in infiltration. Next to her was **Clint Barton**, a.k.a. **Hawkeye**, not just the best archer in the world but also well versed in several forms of combat.

Across from Hawkeye were the Twins—two young Avengers who had recently joined the team and who had incredible powers. Pietro Maximoff—Quicksilver—could move with superhuman speed, and his sister, **Wanda Maximoff—the Scarlet Witch**—could use magic powers to blast back enemies.

Rounding out the team was **Vision**, an android built with a digital intelligence so advanced that he was actually a form of artificial life. Vision had superhuman strength and superhuman reflexes, as well as the abilities to phase through solid walls, shoot powerful beams, and repair himself when injured.

"What's the story, Sam? Why the emergency message?" asked Hawkeye.

Sam used holo-display to help get his teammates up to speed on the possible threat from space.

"So what will we need to do if Iron Man and the others find this

Thanos guy?" asked the Scarlet Witch *NERVOUSLY*.

"We're just going to have to wait for news from the advanced team," responded Falcon, "but the Avengers have beaten Thanos before, so we know we can again." Falcon cleared his throat after saying the villain's name. Thanos was feared by everyone, including this Avenger.

"Okay. We wait for information. . . . What do we do in the meantime?" asked Widow.

Falcon had been expecting this question. This group of world-saving heroes—this group of Avengers—was looking to **HIM** for leadership. Everything had been happening so quickly that Falcon hadn't had time to put together a plan, but he was quick on his feet.

"I was thinking of something like this . . ." said Sam as he presented a rotating patrol schedule that gave every Avenger duties and also time in the training room, as well as time off.

"With the others out in space, there's more world for each of us to protect," admitted Sam, "but I know that if we work together, we can handle it."

Quicksilver reviewed Sam's plan, highly pleased with his organizational skills. "Yeah, I think we can do this," he confirmed.

Even Vision was impressed: "Your proposal operates at near-peak proficiency, Sam Wilson." That was really high praise, coming from the android.

As the Avengers ended their meeting and headed off to take care of their various responsibilities, Falcon smiled. He was starting to feel pretty good about this whole **"leadership"** thing. Maybe Cap was right: maybe he was a natural leader.

SCHEDULE

PATROL
SCARLET WITCH	14:00 HRS
BLACK WIDOW	14:00 HRS
QUICKSILVER	15:00 HRS
FALCON	16:00 HRS

TRAINING ROOM PRACTICE
BLACK WIDOW	9:00 HRS
HAWKEYE	11:00 HRS
QUICKSILVER	11:00 HRS
VISON	12:00 HRS
SCARLET WITCH	13:00 HRS

CHAPTER 4

*T*he next morning Sam woke to loud shouting coming from the common room. He stumbled out of bed, throwing on his wing-pack. What could it be? Could villains have broken into the Avengers Tower? **Were they under attack?**

But it was nothing of the sort. Sam arrived to find Quicksilver and Hawkeye involved in a screaming match.

"WHAT'S GOING ON HERE?"

Sam asked with genuine surprise as he stepped between the two angry Avengers. Amid the shouted insults, Sam pieced the story together. It turned out Sam's rotating schedule had them both using the training room that morning, and the two couldn't agree on which program to use, target practice or speed practice. The argument started small but quickly heated up to personal insults.

GIMME!

"Your practice schedule, that's what caused all this?" asked Falcon.

"I've got to keep up my skills," said Hawkeye, waving his bow.

"You sure do. In fact, let's see how well you do without that thing," said Quicksilver, zipping up at a blurring speed, yanking Hawkeye's bow away from him, and racing around the room with it.

"Hey, give me that!" shouted Hawkeye. "I may not be able to keep up with you, but I can aim more than an arrow!" He started throwing vases, lamps, and anything else he could get his hands on at Quicksilver.

shouted Sam. **"You're behaving like children!"**

"Wait. . . . Do you hear something?" asked Quicksilver.

Sure enough, they all heard more shouting coming from the hallway, but this time it was female voices. Within seconds the door slammed open and in came Black Widow and the Scarlet Witch, yelling at each other.

YOU'RE SUPPOSED TO USE YOUR POWERS ON THE BAD GUYS, WANDA. NOT YOUR ALLIES. IT'S CALLED TEAMWORK. YOU MIGHT WANT TO TRY IT SOMETIME!

"Now what?"

Sam asked them.

Like the schedule said they should be, both Black Widow and the Scarlet Witch were out on patrol when the gang of villains known as the **Wrecking Crew** were spotted battling a few police officers. Widow and Scarlet Witch both responded, trying to help. The only problem? They both went after the Wrecking Crew's leader, **Bulldozer**. The Scarlet Witch threw a hex at Bulldozer, but it missed and hit the nearby Widow instead.

TEAMWORK ALSO MEANS NOT BLOCKING YOUR PARTNER'S SHOTS, I BET!

The Wrecking Crew were eventually caught, but according to Widow, the situation could have turned out much worse.

"WANDA WASN'T WATCHING OUT FOR ME," Widow complained to Sam. **"I NEED TEAMMATES WHO HAVE MY BACK, NOT ONES WHO SHOOT AT MY BACK!"**

"IT WASN'T MY FAULT!" shouted the Scarlet Witch. **"WIDOW JUMPED IN WHERE SHE WASN'T NEEDED AND CROSSED MY LINE OF FIRE!"**

"WHERE SHE 'WASN'T NEEDED'?"

asked Hawkeye incredulously. **"BLACK WIDOW'S ALWAYS NEEDED IN A FIGHT,"** he continued, clearly taking Widow's side.

"IF MY SISTER SAYS IT WASN'T HER FAULT, THEN IT WASN'T HER FAULT," shouted Quicksilver, sticking up for the Scarlet Witch.

Before long, Vision entered, watching the whole argument in confusion. It was clear that he didn't understand these very human conflicts.

Soon the argument turned into a four-way shouting fight, with Sam trying to calm everyone down—but he wasn't even able to make himself heard over everyone else!

Oh, man ... *What would Cap do in this situation?* Sam asked himself.

But before he could figure it out, the Tower's **alarm** went off so loudly that everyone stopped and turned to check the wall screen.

"What's the situation, Jarvis?" Sam asked the computer.

"I'm afraid it's a red alert, sir," reported the disembodied voice of Jarvis. "Ultron is using his robot troops to attack somewhere in the city!"

Ultron? *The evil robot bent on destroying all of mankind?*

Oh, great ...

CHAPTER

5

Vibranium

"*A*vengers. . .assemble!" shouted Falcon as he, Black Widow, Hawkeye, Quicksilver, the Scarlet Witch, and Vision gathered in front of **Horizon Labs**. He'd always wanted to be the one to shout that famous Avengers catch-phrase, but under these circumstances it just wasn't as cool as he'd hoped it'd be.

"Scans are useless," reported Vision as he attempted to use his enhanced eyesight to see inside the building. "There's something blocking me."

"Well, I guess we know where they went in," said Hawkeye, checking out a massive breach in the side of the building.

"But that's not how they're going to come out," shouted Quicksilver as he slipped toward the building at super *SPEED.*

"Quicksilver, wait!" Falcon shouted after the fleet-footed Avenger, but it was too late. Moving at almost the speed of sound, Quicksilver was already inside the building.

"Doesn't your brother know not to run off on his own during a team mission?" Black Widow demanded of the Scarlet Witch. "If he were a **S.H.I.E.L.D.** agent, he'd be brought up on charges for taking off like that while under orders."

"Don't start quoting **S.H.I.E.L.D.** regulations to me," the Scarlet Witch said, bristling. "Where we grew up there were no 'rules of engagement.'. . . There was only survival."

Black Widow took a step toward Scarlet

Witch, but before she could argue, Falcon stepped between the two.

"Avengers! Stop focusing on each other! The real enemy is inside, and he's not—" But before Falcon could finish, there was a loud crash, followed by Quicksilver's body flying through one of the lab's front windows and landing hard on the pavement at their feet.

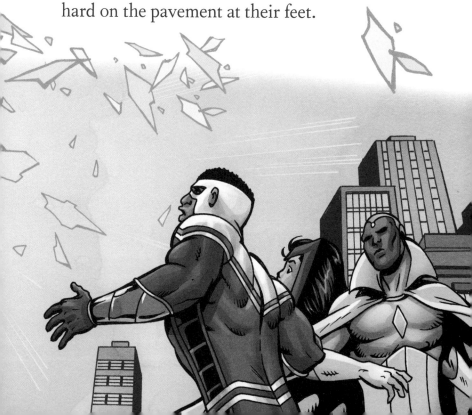

"Pietro! Are you okay?" shouted the Scarlet Witch as she dropped to her brother's side.

"He is okay but unconscious," reported Vision, scanning Quicksilver's body.

Suddenly a hail of laser-fire from inside the building sprayed around the Avengers, causing all the heroes to scatter and dive for cover.

Out of the building burst a half dozen identical Ultron units, robot soldiers that Ultron controlled and operated by remote.

"Ah, humanity's so-called heroes. . . How pathetic," laughed Ultron as he emerged from the building behind his troops. With him were a few more units, all carrying boxes marked **"VIBRANIUM."**

Ultron continued his rant. "Don't

you know by now that humanity is long since outdated? An update is coming!"

As soon as Falcon saw the boxes of Vibranium, he realized Ultron's plan. Vibranium was an extremely rare metal found in the African nation of **Wakanda**. Cap's shield was mostly made out of Vibranium, because the metal was able to absorb any vibrations or energy directed at it. If Ultron managed to coat his robot army with a skin of this rare metal, it would be practically indestructible. Nothing could stop it from marching across the face of the country, and eventually the world!

"Avengers, we can't let Ultron get away with those boxes," shouted Falcon to the other heroes. "Time to get on the defensive!"

Following Falcon's lead, the Avengers jumped into action. Widow **bounced** and **leapt,** getting behind the line of Ultron units, and unleashed **intense** fire from her wrist-mounted stinger weapons.

Nearby, Hawkeye fired off a **series of** trick arrows—explosive arrows, net arrows, oil-slick arrows—**throwing** everything he had at the robots!

At the same time, Vision confronted one of the troops, **wrestling** it and **blasting** it with his eye blasts.

Falcon took to the air, swooping in and firing from above. His maneuvers drew the attention of a few of the troops, letting the Scarlet Witch get close to Ultron unchallenged, where she loosed magical fire that burst around the maniacal villain!

I think we got this, Falcon thought, watching his team take down the bad guys and realizing that Cap would be proud of their performance.

But seconds later, everything went wrong!

Hawkeye, having just brought down two of Ultron's robot troops, turned and fired an ice arrow at Ultron. But at the same moment, one of the Scarlet Witch's beams blasted across the field of fire, bouncing Hawkeye's arrow back toward him! Seeing this, Widow jumped forward, attempting to shoot the arrow out of the sky, but instead she fired too soon and hit the

Scarlet Witch. The Scarlet Witch shouted in pain and fell on the ground. Vision broke off from his fight to run to the Scarlet Witch's side.

At that moment, Hawkeye's ricocheting arrow came right at him and popped, covering him with an instant-freeze fluid that encased him in a shell of ice!

"Excellent!" shouted Ultron as he grabbed the frozen Hawkeye and lifted him up. "You bumbling excuses for Avengers do my work for me. This Avenger is an added prize that I didn't expect to win! Thank you, all."

Ultron and the robot

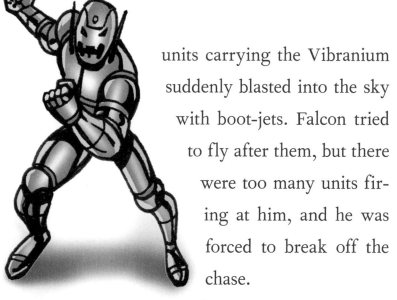

units carrying the Vibranium suddenly blasted into the sky with boot-jets. Falcon tried to fly after them, but there were too many units firing at him, and he was forced to break off the chase.

Within seconds Ultron was gone... and he had both a cache of indestructible metal and one of their teammates with him.

CHAPTER 6

Back at the Tower, the customary mission **"debriefing"** quickly became a shouting match. Black Widow yelled at the Scarlet Witch for deflecting Hawkeye's arrow back in his direction, and the Scarlet Witch yelled at Widow for hitting her with stings.

"Did you do that on purpose?" the Scarlet Witch demanded of Widow. "I accidentally hit you when we were fighting the Wrecking Crew, and so you thought you'd pay me back or something?"

"Of course not," responded Widow, offended. "I was acting quickly to try to fix your mistake by blowing that arrow out of the air!"

Even Quicksilver and Vision had a heated exchange, or at least as heated as Vision ever got. Quicksilver declared that Vision should have been able to see inside the building, making it unnecessary for Quicksilver to run inside, but Vision pointed out that no one ordered Quicksilver to run inside blind—he'd done it on his own.

"Protocol dictates awaiting approval before entering an enemy site," Vision pointed out.

Quicksilver just rolled his eyes. **"Pft. . . protocol. . ."**

Sam tried to control the discussion, but getting anyone's attention in all the fuss seemed to be impossible. Finally, he shouted at the top of his lungs:

Suddenly quieted, everyone turned and looked toward Sam in total surprise. Sam never shouted like that.

"There's only one person to blame for what happened today," said Sam before pausing. Everyone leaned in, interested to see which side of the argument their temporary leader would come down on.

"The person to blame. . .is me.
With more guidance and better leadership, you all would have won that battle. . . and Hawkeye would be safe."

Sam felt like everything would have been different if Cap were there on Earth leading them, instead of on that space mission. *What would Cap have done differently?* he thought. Sam didn't know, but he did know that Cap hardly ever made mistakes. *In fact, maybe Cap's only mistake was leaving me in charge*, he thought.

After Sam's statement, everyone felt awkward. They didn't continue the argument, but they didn't resolve it, either.

"I guess it doesn't matter whose fault it was," said Widow. "Either way Hawkeye is gone. . . **and I'm going to find a way to bring him back**."

"Right," said Quicksilver. "When do we head out to look for him? I could race around the state in a grid pattern and—"

"Not 'we,' just me," interrupted Widow. "Hawkeye's my old partner from **S.H.I.E.L.D.**, and he's my responsibility. I'm used to doing operations on my own. I don't need anyone from this team to get in my way. . .or to shoot me in the back," she finished, looking right at the Scarlet Witch.

Before anyone could reply, Widow turned on her heel and stormed out of the room. Everyone else looked back at Sam.

"**She can just do that?** Go off on her own like that?" asked Quicksilver.

"This isn't the military, this is the Avengers. She can do whatever she wants," replied Sam.

"**But...what do we do?** Should we just let her go?" asked the Scarlet Witch.

HMPH

Sam looked back at them. This was what it meant to be the leader. The team asked questions, and Sam had to be prepared to answer them. It was what Cap was counting on him to do....

But Sam didn't have an answer ready. What would Cap do if one of his teammates had been kidnapped and another one was planning on going solo to get him back?

After a pause, Sam spoke again.

"I—I don't know what we should do," he admitted. It wasn't a very good answer, but it was the **truth**. "Just give me some time to think," said Sam, and then he, too, left the room.

The Twins, **shocked**, looked at each other in confusion. Vision, on the other hand, just watched Sam leave, a look of concern on his face.

CHAPTER 7

Sam took the elevator straight to the roof of Avengers Tower, extended his Falcon wings, and jumped off the edge. New York City looked so beautiful from above, glass from skyscrapers glinting in the sun like jewels.

But Sam couldn't enjoy the view knowing that somewhere there was an evil robot villain, holding an Avenger hostage—a friend.

Even if he knew where Ultron was, even if he knew how to stop him, he couldn't. If his team wouldn't listen to him, how could he lead them into a dangerous mission? More Avengers could be kidnapped **...or worse!**

Before long Sam found himself landing at his favorite thinking spot, a perch on the top of the **Empire State Building**.

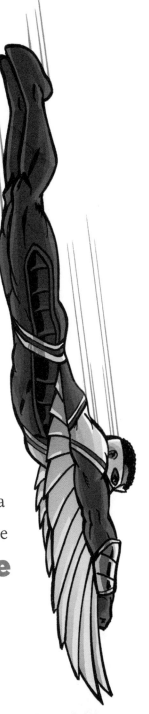

There he sat, looking out into space, imagining what Cap would say if he knew how badly Sam's first attempt at leadership had gone.

"I hope I am not disturbing you," said Vision as he suddenly phased through the wall behind Sam.

"Augh!" shouted Sam in surprise. Vision's ability to pass through solid objects could be downright spooky! "You scared me half to death."

"Apologies, Sam Wilson," said Vision. **"I came to offer you one cent in exchange for your ideas."**

"The phrase is 'a penny for your thoughts,'" Sam said, correcting the android.

"Did I not just express that same meaning?" asked Vision.

"Yes, I suppose the words you used meant

the same thing"—Sam shrugged—"but it's a saying, and the saying is 'A penny for your thoughts.'"

"There is much about human communication that I still do not understand," admitted Vision.

"Well...that's true of me, too, I guess," Sam admitted, "judging by what happened today."

"I wanted to ask you about that," said Vision. "The Avengers are all on the same side, yet they seem to be caught up in nonproductive verbal disputes. Why do they not get along?"

"Yeah, that's just humans," explained Sam. "Most of us want to get along with others, but sometimes personalities just clash. That's why a team needs a good leader to bring them together. If I were a better leader, like Cap, we wouldn't be having this problem."

"Why did Captain America put you in charge of the team if you are incapable of being a good leader?" asked Vision.

"I was just asking myself that," admitted Falcon. "Cap is a natural leader, so maybe he just thought he saw the same thing in me. . . . But he was wrong. I don't always know what to do, like Cap."

"Correction: Captain America didn't always know what to do," stated Vision.

"Yes, he did," said Falcon. **"Hello . . . that's why he's Cap!"**

"I'm sorry to contradict you, Sam Wilson, but I have all of Captain Steve Rogers's military records, and I can demonstrate to you that your statement is false. . . ."

With that, Vision raised his palm and projected a hologram of a slightly younger-looking Captain America.

Sam leaned in and looked closely, focusing all of his attention as the hologram started talking.

War journal, day forty-three: We're trapped behind enemy lines, and I just don't know what to do. . . .

CHAPTER 8

*I*t was 1943, and Captain America was leading his elite team of soldiers, known as the Howling Commandos, on a raid deep into enemy territory when their plane was spotted and shelled down by Hydra antiaircraft weapons.

Miraculously, Dum Dum Dugan, one of the Howling Commandos, was able to bring the plane in for a crash landing, but it was way more "crash" than it was "landing."

The commandos barely survived. All of them were injured in some way, ranging from cuts and scrapes to broken bones.

"We're behind enemy lines, near a Hydra installation, and some of us are too injured to travel," reported Cap in his private war journal. "This is one of my first missions as team leader, and everyone is asking me what to do. . . . To be honest, I'm not sure what to tell them. Should we attempt to make it back to our base on foot? Or will that make us too much of a target? Maybe we should just dig in here, hide, and wait for a rescue mission."

Cap's next journal entry was even direr. Some of the Howling Commandos, not getting any direction from Cap, were thinking about striking out on their own. Others refused to travel. It was getting more desperate by the minute.

"I'm filled with doubts," Cap admitted to his war journal. *"I thought that I was ready to lead this team, but maybe I'm not. Maybe I'm just not cut out to be a leader at all."*

But in his darkest moment, Cap found a picture of himself with Dr. Abraham Erskine and Howard Stark, the two brilliant scientists who had created the Super-Soldier process that gave Cap his special abilities.

"Looking at that photo gave me hope," reported Cap. "If those two great men believed in me enough to trust me, then I must be able to do the things they need me to do."

With determination, Cap searched for a solution. While checking the map, he realized that the nearby Hydra base held fighter planes. The Commandos might

be too injured to make it all the way back to home base on foot, but he knew they could make it as far as the Hydra base.

The Commandos who were less injured helped move the more seriously injured ones, and in a daring mission, they snuck into the Hydra base, stole a plane, and flew it back to safety!

That experience led Cap to an important conclusion. **Half of leadership,** he realized, **was about believing in yourself and believing in your team.**

As Vision's hologram ended, Sam was surprised. "Cap had to *learn* to be a leader?" he asked. "I always assumed that he was a natural leader."

Vision considered this. "Maybe even a natural leader sometimes has difficult moments. Maybe what makes them 'naturals' is that they never give up trying, even when they most want to."

Falcon realized that Vision was right. **"Come on, Vision, we've got to go,"** he said, extending his wings.

"Where are we going?" asked the android.

"Back to Avengers Tower. I've got a team to lead."

Sam got back to Avengers Tower just as Black Widow was heading out on her solo attempt to locate and free Hawkeye. Quicksilver and the Scarlet Witch were quietly watching her go, not sure whether they wanted her to stay or not.

"Wait," said Sam as he and Vision entered. "You're not going anywhere."

Widow spun around to face Sam, looking angry. "Who's going to stop me? You? I'm not sitting around here. I'm going after Clint."

"Yes, you are going after him," said Sam. **"We all are. And we're doing it as a team!"**

This took everyone by surprise.

"Look," said Sam, now with the room's full attention. "I know I haven't been the best leader so far. But the Avengers were originally formed because there came a day, unlike any other, when Earth's Mightiest Heroes found themselves united against a common threat . . . and today, Ultron is that kind of threat.

"If the team were to split apart now, Ultron would be halfway to victory," Sam pointed out. "So far our team has been focusing on the things that separate us, but now it's time to focus on what unites us: our duty to the planet!"

Everyone looked around the room, realizing that Sam was right. They nodded in agreement at each other.

"Okay," said Widow. **"But how do we find Ultron?"**

Sam smiled.

"That's where my latest invention is going to come in handy," he said with a grin. **"Follow me. . . ."**

CHAPTER

9

Redwing's helmet

"**A** little small for you, isn't it?" asked Widow, looking at the tiny helmet in Sam's hands. They were now in Iron Man's lab, and Sam was showing the rest of the team the invention he'd been working on for the past several months. The helmet was sleek and aerodynamic but had wires and electrodes running along the sides of it.

"It's not for me," Sam replied with a smile as he led them to the roof.

"This is Redwing." He opened a massive birdcage and brought out a beautiful bird, a wild falcon with flaming orange, almost red, plumage. "I found him sick in Rio and nursed him back to health. I trained him."

"Your invention is headgear for a bird?" asked Quicksilver, confused.

"Not just any headgear," Sam replied. "This helmet links me to Redwing. Everything Redwing sees gets transferred to the display in my visor."

"You turned your pet bird into a webcam?" asked the Scarlet Witch.

"Not just a webcam," pointed out Widow. "A *spy* cam. Redwing would be perfect for covert intelligence gathering."

"How can this help us locate Hawkeye?" asked Vision.

"It helps because it doesn't stop with just Redwing," explained Falcon. "Redwing acts as a transceiver, broadcasting what he sees, but he also acts as a receiver. Through him I can actually detect the neurological impulses of other birds within his range."

"Meaning what, exactly?" asked the Scarlet Witch.

"Meaning when Redwing has this on, I can see everything that is seen by any bird for miles around," said Sam.

"But there are thousands and thousands of birds in the city," pointed out Quicksilver.

"All the better to hunt Ultron with," remarked Widow.

"Basically, you're trying to get all the birds of New York to work together as a team?" asked the Scarlet Witch.

"That's right! This is my first test of the system," said Sam as he fitted the little helmet on the obedient Redwing. **"Fly, Redwing!** Show me what you see." Then Sam released the bird into the sky.

Instantly, inside Sam's visor a window popped open showing him a bird's-eye view of the city. "Huh," said Sam. "I only have

Redwing's transmission, not any other—" But before he could finish his thought, thousands of new windows started popping open, showing him views from every single angle of Manhattan!

"It's working!" Sam shouted, pleased.

Within an hour, Sam's visor computer had sorted through the images from the birds and was searching for signs of Ultron. Soon after that, the computer flagged an image seen by a pigeon under a bridge in a warehouse district north of the city. In the shot Sam could clearly see some of Ultron's robots entering a supposedly abandoned building through a side door.

"We've got him," Sam announced to the team.

Once they arrived at the building, Widow popped the lock, and the team snuck inside.

Sure enough, the members of Ultron's robot army

were walking the corridors, but using stealth, the Avengers took out several of them without being seen and made their way to a darkened computer center deep inside the building.

"Can you hack into these, Vision?" Sam asked as he pointed to the racks of computers. "Any information you find could give us a clue about the best way to take Ultron down."

"I can utilize any system," said Vision as he raised his hand to one of the terminals. Soon he was downloading the data from Ultron's hard drives. "This data requires your attention," Vision said, pointing to some information on a screen.

Sam bent in closer and took a look. He couldn't believe it. "According to this, there was no signal from space!"

"What do you mean?" asked the Scarlet Witch.

"Thanos isn't putting together an army in space. The evidence was all set up by Ultron!" explained Sam. **"Iron Man, Cap, and the others are on a wild goose chase. There's nothing up there for them to find!"**

"That's right!" came a booming voice from outside the room. "I knew that if I could trick the core Avengers into leaving the planet, Earth would be mine for the taking. . . . After all, the *inferior* Avengers units left behind could be easily beaten."

With that Ultron stepped into the room, surrounded by his robot troops.

"'Inferior'?" Sam looked at Ultron calmly, no fear in his eyes, and then turned to his team and said simply, **"Let's show Ultron who's inferior. . . . Avengers: ASSEMBLE!"**

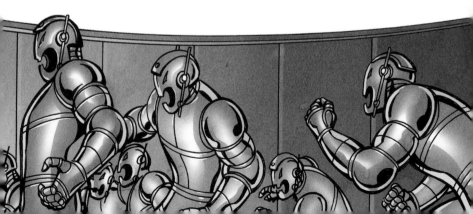

CHAPTER 10

*T*he fight was intense and brutal. Ultron's robots sprang on the Avengers, hacking, slashing, and blasting like the remorseless machines of destruction they were designed to be!

But if Ultron was counting on the team being as disorganized as they'd been during the fight at Horizon Labs, he was sorely disappointed.

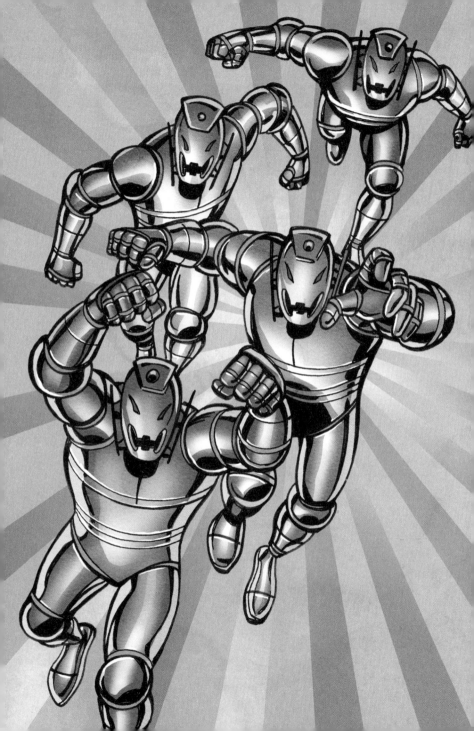

"Cover Vision," directed Falcon, sending Widow, Quicksilver, and the Scarlet Witch straight into combat. **"Vision, get Hawkeye's location from Ultron's computer."**

Widow jumped, kicked, and fired stings while the Scarlet Witch fell in behind her, shooting left and right, but being careful to always keep Widow in view.

At the same time, Quicksilver sped around Ultron himself, whipping up a whirlwind that prevented Ultron from even being able to shoot.

As soon as Vision got Hawkeye's location from the computer, Falcon called out a new plan of attack. He sent Vision to phase through Ultron's robots, smashing them, while the Scarlet Witch's magical hexes protected Black Widow's escape.

Widow made her way to Hawkeye and used her lock-picking skills to free the archer. Once Hawkeye was free, Sam ordered him to provide cover fire to support Quicksilver. With Hawkeye backing him, Quicksilver smashed robot after robot.

Soon all that was left was Ultron himself.

"This does not compute," exclaimed Ultron. "You are supposed to be the weak members of the Avengers. . . ."

"A team is only as weak as its leader," said Widow.

"And we've got a strong leader," said Hawkeye, looking at Falcon. "I can see that now."

"Thanks, Hawkeye. Thanks, team." Falcon smiled as he slashed his wing-blades across Ultron's circuits, shutting the maniacal robot down for good. They quickly called in **S.H.I.E.L.D.**, whose agents hauled Ultron off to a top-secret prison designed specifically for Super Villains of his caliber.

AAHHKK!

Later, the *QUINJET* zoomed past the moon toward Earth, ready to reenter the atmosphere.

"Hurry," Captain America urged Iron Man, who was in the pilot's seat. "We need to get back and help the other Avengers!"

"I'm pushing this thing as fast as I can, Cap," responded Iron Man.

Once they had reached the edge of the solar system and seen that there was no army out there, Cap, Iron Man, Hulk, and Thor quickly realized that the signal had been faked. They didn't know who had done it, but they did know it meant that Falcon and the others were in trouble!

Soon the **QUINJET** docked at Avengers Tower. Cap and the others rushed inside and were shocked by what they found:

the rest of the team was . . . **calmly hanging out, enjoying one another's company**!

Hawkeye was giving tips to Quicksilver on how to aim for the bull's-eye as they played darts.

On the other side of the room, the Scarlet Witch and Black Widow were having a bite of lunch together while talking about their favorite locations in Eastern Europe. It turned out they both had been to many of the same places.

Meanwhile, Sam was giving Vision a closer look at the helmet for Redwing. Vision was suitably impressed with the invention.

Everyone looked up as Cap and the others came running in. "Sam, the signal from space, it was a—" started Cap.

But Sam finished Cap's sentence for him, saying, "A trick. We know. Ultron did it. Don't worry, we took care of it." Sam shrugged it off like it was no big deal. "Hey, you guys hungry? We made tacos."

Cap and Iron Man looked at each other, relieved. Their concern had clearly been unnecessary. Falcon had it all taken care of.

"I like tacos," said Iron Man.

That evening Cap was back in the Avengers training room, waiting patiently in the simulated redwood forest's treetops. Sam had asked to make another attempt at beating Cap in the "capture the flag" training exercise, but it looked like Sam was going to lose again.

Cap saw Sam jump from the underbrush and head toward his flag, but Cap sprang into action. "Sorry, Sam, not this time," said Cap as

he again tackled Sam in midair, taking him to the ground.

"I wouldn't be so sure about that," said Sam, pointing up at the place where Cap's flag was hidden.

Cap looked up just in time to see Black Widow and the Scarlet Witch grabbing his flag and waving it around.

"We did it!" whooped the Scarlet Witch.

Cap was pleasantly surprised. No team had ever beaten him at capture the flag . . . until then. Good for them!

"It's like you said, Cap," explained Falcon. "This can be a leadership exercise, too."

"That's true," said Cap. "I've said it once, and I'll say it again: Sam, **you're a natural leader.**"

STARRING

STAR-LORD

BY CHRIS "DOC" WYATT

ILLUSTRATED BY
RON LIM AND ANDY TROY

FEATURING YOUR FAVORITES!

STAR-LORD

CAPTAIN MARVEL

COSMO

GAMORA

ROCKET

GROOT

DRAX

ORLANI

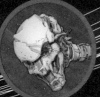

KNOWHERE

EARTH

THE SKRULL

STAR-LORD'S SHIP

SHI'AR

YON-ROGG

ULTIMATE NULLIFIER

ROBOTIC LIONS?!?

THE STORY OF STAR-LORD

*E*ven when **PETER QUILL** was a little boy on Earth, he always defended people in need. If someone was being picked on at school, Peter stood up for them, even if it meant getting in fights with bullies who were bigger than he was. Peter just seemed to have been born with a strong sense of justice.

When he was a little older, Peter finally learned from his mother the truth about his father. Peter's dad was from another planet, called Spartax. His father and mother had met and fallen in love when his father's ship had crashed on Earth.

Knowing that he had a father out in the galaxy drove Peter to reach for the stars. He studied hard in school, designed his own spaceship, and eventually took off from Earth to explore the galaxy!

Many things were very different on the alien worlds Peter visited, but one thing remained the same. . . . Wherever Peter went he found that there was always some bully who wanted to pick on the little guys. Peter wasn't going to let that happen, no matter what planet he happened to be on.

Peter chose to be a hero! He became—

!

While fighting to protect the innocent, Star-Lord joined with other heroes from other parts of the cosmos, and together this group became known as the

CHAPTER 1

*F*or the earthling known as **Peter Quill**, life was pretty good onboard the space station ***Knowhere***. It was an amazing place, after all. Unlike normal space stations, it wasn't made out of metal or a rare space element. It was made out of bone!

How was that possible? The station was built inside the skull of a long-dead giant celestial being. "I live inside a massive floating alien skull," Peter would say. "How cool is THAT?!"

The station was filled with strange and wonderful beings. Peter got to meet people and do things that no other human being ever had, or ever would. It was a pretty special feeling.

But the very best thing about Knowhere was that it served as home base for the

an intergalactic Super Hero team that Peter was proud to be a part of!

There were four other members of the team: **Drax**, the green-skinned, alien strongman; **GROOT**, a living tree monster from space; **Rocket**, a furry little weapons specialist who looked almost exactly like a large Earth raccoon; and **GAMORA**, an intergalactic warrior trained in several dozen forms of combat. And, of course, there was the leader of the group,

.

When he wasn't out in space doing awesome (if sometimes super-dangerous) missions with his team, Peter spent his time doing fun stuff on Knowhere. Take today for example:

This morning Peter went
to the Celestial Boot
(a restaurant where the
Guardians love to hang
out) and played space
darts with Rocket. "This
is going to be a bull's-eye,"
Rocket shouted as he held up his dart.

"But you're not even aiming at the
target," Peter pointed out, holding his
dart up as well.

"You'll see," Rocket said. He released his dart, and it zipped around the room, **bouncing** off walls and knocking over people's drinks before landing dead in the target's center.

> HEY, HOW DID YOU DO THAT?

Rocket showed Peter a tiny device on the tip of his dart. **"Homing beacon,"** Rocket explained. "It will always go where I tell it to, no matter what direction I throw it in— I designed it myself!"

WHOOSH!

"Always?" asked Peter. "Let's see about that!" He took the whole box of darts and threw them all at once, scattering them in the air! The darts WHOOSHED around the restaurant in all directions, causing patrons to duck as they pinged and ponged off the plates, the tables, the floor, and the ceiling before...

...all landed, clustered perfectly, in the bull's-eye of the target!

"AWESOME!"

shouted Peter and Rocket together, high-fiving.

Later that day, Peter hung out with all of his other friends.

He did a space race with **Drax**, ran some cool **ZERO-G** training exercises with **Gamora**, and even tried meditating in a garden with **Groot**.

WOO-HOO!

I'M LIGHT AS AIR!

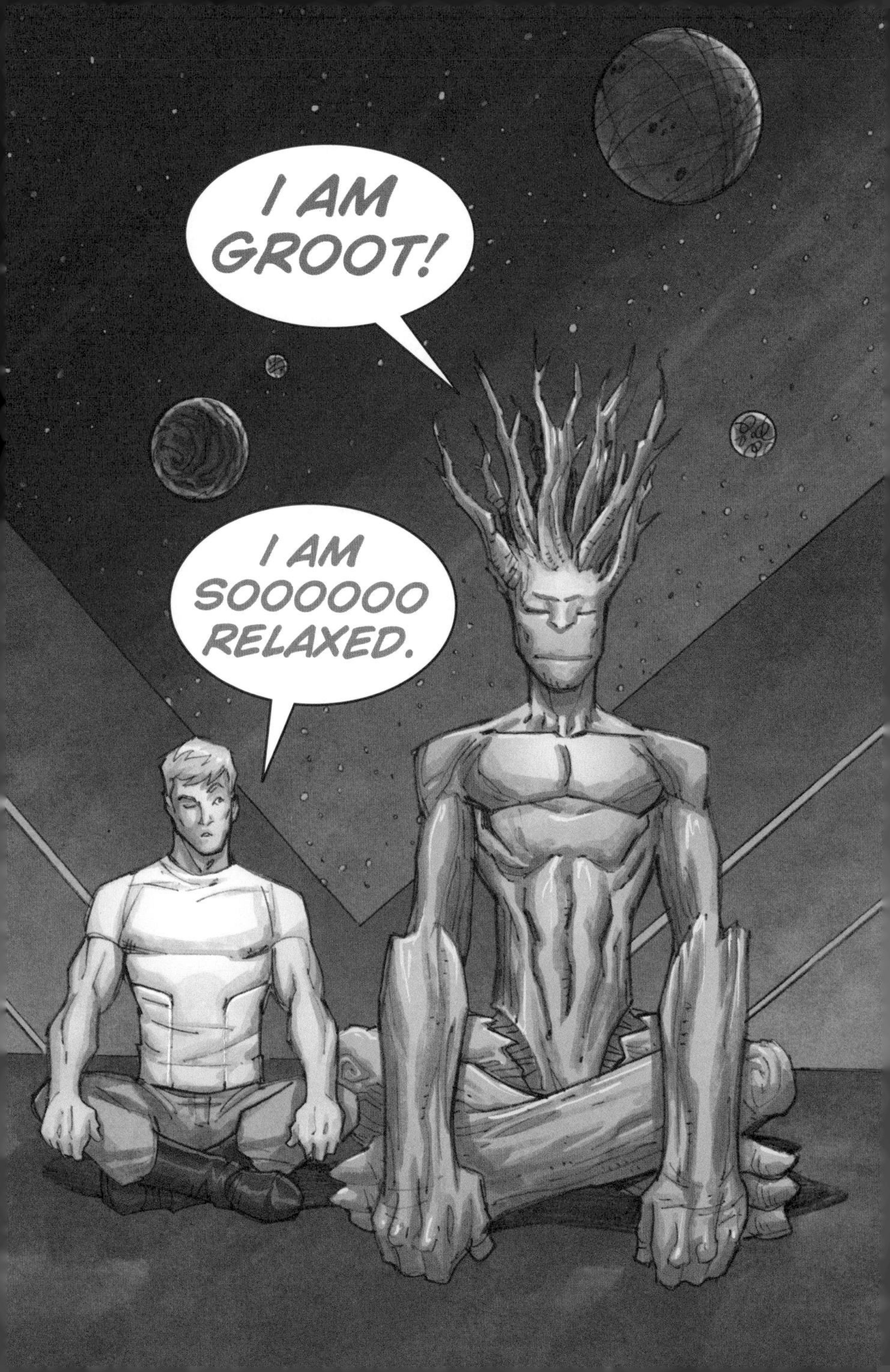
I AM GROOT!
I AM SOOOOOO RELAXED.

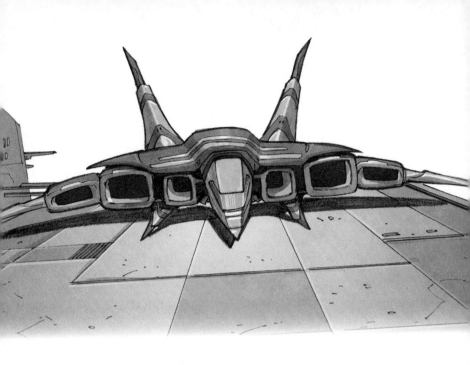

All in all, it was a pretty incredible day. When it was over, Peter headed back home to his bedroom on board his spaceship, which was docked semipermanently on Knowhere. On his way he walked past the only other earthling living on Knowhere: Cosmo.

"Good evening, Peter," Cosmo said as he walked past Peter going in the other direction down a sidewalk.

"You too, Cosmo," said Peter to the animal. Cosmo was the only other earthling, but Cosmo wasn't a human being. He was a dog! Born in Russia in the 1960s, Cosmo was launched into the galaxy as a cosmonaut, part of the Russian government's experiments in space travel. But Cosmo fell into a wormhole, and he wound up gaining advanced intelligence and mental abilities—including the power to communicate with humans. Now he was head of security on Knowhere.

OH, BY THE WAY. . . HAPPY BIRTHDAY, PETER!

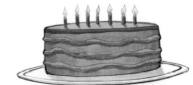

That stopped Peter in his tracks. "What?"

"I know that the calendar is different here on Knowhere," said Cosmo. "The days and weeks are different lengths, and there are only eight months in the year and everything. . . .But I keep an Earth calendar on my desk at work, because it reminds me of home, and I happened to notice that on Earth, right now, it's your birthday."

It was Peter's birthday and he hadn't even realized it!

SAY WHAAAAA?

CHAPTER

2

*P*eter was bummed out. Back on Earth, he'd loved his birthdays. His mother had always made a lot of fuss for Peter on what she called his "big day." There was a party filled with cake, music, and, of course, presents. But more than anything else, there was that warm feeling of being surrounded by friends and family

who clearly loved him and wanted to make things special on his "big day."

And now, so far from home, Peter didn't even notice that his birthday was happening. It had been years since Peter had gone back to Earth to see anyone he remembered. Yep, there was no denying it— **Peter was homesick**.

The next day Peter's friends the Guardians, could tell he was down, and they tried to cheer him up. Rocket and Groot took him to the **Orlani races**.

"Nobody can feel bad at the Orlani races," declared Rocket.

Orlani

141

"I am Groot," Groot agreed with a slight nod. He really was agreeing with Rocket, but all he ever said was "I am Groot." His best friend, Rocket, always knew what he meant anyway.

"See? He agrees with me," Rocket confirmed.

Orlani were little creatures—kind of like the alien versions of muskrats or ferrets. For fun, the Orlani were put in little tracks and on "go," they raced each other toward the finish line as the spectators watched and cheered them on! Everyone picked their favorites and cheered them on.

When the race started, Rocket shouted,

"Run, Little Brownie!"

at the Orlani he liked. **"I am Groot,"** Groot shouted, also trying to encourage Little Brownie.

Despite himself, Peter started to cheer up. But then Little Brownie JUMPED out of the track, and ran straight into the crowd.

"Hey, where's it going?" Peter asked. Suddenly, he felt something weird. Little Brownie was running straight up the leg of Peter's pants!

"Ahh— Ohhh— Awww—"

Peter shouted as he jumped around! The Orlani's little claws were scratching and tickling him all at once! "Get this thing off of meeeee!" Peter yelled at Rocket and Groot!

It took several minutes to get the Orlani out of his pants, and the job involved Peter stripping down to his boxers and tank top in public. When it was all over, Peter was in a worse mood than ever.

"OKAY, I WAS WRONG," Rocket admitted. **"SOME PEOPLE MIGHT BE ABLE TO FEEL BAD AT THE ORLANI RACES."**

Peter's friends didn't give up trying to cheer him up. Gamora took Peter to the space dojo to show him some cool new fighting moves. But when Peter tried them, he fell flat on his face!

Later, hoping to treat Peter's homesickness, Drax tried cooking an Earth recipe. There was just one problem: having never made or even tasted Earth food before, Drax got the ingredients all mixed up. He ended up making an **eggplant-chocolate-chicken cake with oyster frosting**. Which, while disgusting to Peter, just so happened to be something Rocket ENJOYED eating!

"Thanks for trying," Peter said to Drax—once he stopped gagging.

VOILA!

Cosmo told Peter that he had just gotten a shipment of **"special treats"** from Earth that he always ate when he wanted to be reminded of home. The considerate canine wanted to share one with Peter, which got Star-Lord excited—until the special treats turned out to be **DOG TREATS**.

I should have realized, Peter thought as he politely choked down the dry, bone-shaped animal snack.

It was really nice that everyone wanted to help, but Peter put it to them bluntly: "Since none of you are even human, you just can't

understand what I need." Focusing on his own disappointment, he walked back home to his ship, not realizing that he had just hurt his friends' feelings.

But that evening, while on his parked ship, Peter heard a knock on the door. He opened it and saw the last thing he ever expected to see

ANOTHER HUMAN!!!

It was **Captain Marvel**, a Super Hero from Earth!

"Star-Lord, I'm so happy I found you," she said. "I need your help. In fact, **everyone on Earth needs your help**!"

CHAPTER

3

*P*eter had met Captain Marvel a few times while Iron Man and some of the other Avengers were on a mission against **THANOS**. He knew that Captain Marvel's real name was **Carol Danvers**. She used to be in the United States Air Force, but after receiving an infusion of **ALIEN DNA**, she developed

super powers—including super strength, endurance, stamina, and even the power of flight! She soon joined the AVENGERS and battled alongside Earth's Mightiest Heroes.

Whether she had **part-alien DNA** or not, Peter was so happy to see a fellow human being! He invited her inside immediately.

Once on board his ship, Captain Marvel explained why she was there.

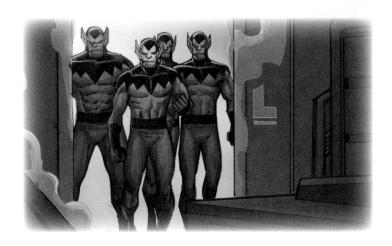

Peter knew the **SKRULLS** all too well. They were aliens, and many of them were evil and loved war. They had tried to invade Earth on multiple occasions but had always been beaten back by the Avengers and other powerful heroes, such as Spider-Man and Wolverine.

"These **SKRULLS** were a small team, and they had been searching for something," Captain Marvel went on. "Eventually the Avengers discovered what the alien agents had been after: the pieces needed to rebuild the. . .

"The Ultimate Nulli-wha?" Peter asked. "Do you mean the weapon capable of destroying entire solar systems?"

Peter had never seen the Ultimate Nullifier, but he knew that even some of the biggest bad guys in the Universe—like GALACTUS, RONAN, and even THANOS himself—were actually afraid of it. To protect the universe, the heroes of Earth had found it and broken it into several pieces, scattering them in secret locations. But if the SKRULLS were able to

put those pieces together again, they'd cause big trouble for sure!

"We captured the whole Skrull team. . .except one," said Captain Marvel.

"Let me guess," Peter replied, a chill going down his spine. "The SKRULL who got away is the one who had the pieces to the Ultimate Nullifier."

"Yes," Captain Marvel confirmed. "And I've tracked him—to planet Knowhere! If that SKRULL agent gets the parts back to his home planet, I'm positive the scientists of his world will be able to put it together again. Once they have a working Ultimate Nullifier, they'll be able to

DESTROY EARTH WITH A SINGLE SHOT!"

The words hit Peter like a ton of bricks. His memories of being a child rushed back: playing kickball in his yard; battling imaginary monsters from his tree house; reading comic books down by the stream. All of these places would be destroyed. His friends—his family—gone. Peter made a **tight fist**. He wasn't going to let that happen. "We have to stop him before it's too late."

"So, you'll help me, Star-Lord?" Captain Marvel asked.

"You bet I will," Peter responded, grabbing his blaster and helmet. **"Where do we start?"**

"Well, that's where it gets tricky," she responded. "Don't forget— SKRULLS are shape-shifters!"

"Oh...right," said Peter, remembering. It was true. Every SKRULL alien had the natural ability to change their bodies and make them look like anyone or anything they wanted. It was a form of camouflage that made them great at their work as spies and secret agents.

"We need to be looking for anyone—or any*thing*—that seems out of place, like they don't belong," said Captain Marvel.

Sometimes I'm the one who feels like I don't belong, Peter thought as he remembered the loneliness he sometimes experienced.

"Sounds like you need to talk to someone who is very familiar with this station and everyone who lives on it," Peter said. "I know just the individual! Someone who knows this place like the back of his hand—well. . .not hand, but paw. . . ."

Captain Marvel gave Peter a confused look.

CHAPTER

4

*E*arly the next morning, Peter picked up Captain Marvel and they went to see **Cosmo** at his office. To Captain Marvel's credit, if she was surprised that the entire space station's security was the responsibility of a talking Earth dog, she didn't show it. But then again, she was probably used to seeing a lot of strange stuff during her work with the Avengers.

"Nice to make your acquaintance, Carol," Cosmo said. "May I call you Carol?"

"Uh, yes, feel free," Captain Marvel responded as she shook Cosmo's paw.

"Thank you. **Would you like some kibble?**" Cosmo asked as he pushed a little dish of dog food across the desk to Captain Marvel.

"Oh, no, thank you," Captain Marvel replied politely.

"So. How can I help you?" asked Cosmo as he gnawed away on a bone.

But before Captain Marvel would say anything about the mission, she told Peter to ask his friend a few questions that only the real Cosmo would know the answer to.

"Where did I get this scratch last week?" asked Peter, pointing to a small abrasion on his arm.

"That probably happened when we were forced to give Rocket a bath," said Cosmo, "on account of those RADIOACTIVE SPACE TICKS that he picked up."

"It's true," Peter confirmed. "Rocket hates baths. He was scratching and biting the whole time."

AIN'T HAPPENIN'!

"Ask him one more, please," Captain Marvel requested. "Just to be sure."

"What game do you like to play in the hologram video game system?" Peter asked.

"THE ONE WHERE YOU GET TO CHASE A MAILMAN WITH ROCKET-BOOTS," Cosmo replied.

It was true. Peter had played that game with him before. It was pretty boring. You just chased the mailman, caught him, and chased him again—over and over.

"That's Cosmo for sure," Peter confirmed.

"Now what's with all the strange questions?" asked Cosmo.

Captain Marvel filled him in about the missing SKRULL agent and the pieces of the Ultimate Nullifier.

"So you asked those questions to make sure a SKRULL hadn't taken my shape and was pretending to be me," Cosmo realized. "Very smart."

Cosmo took the SKRULL threat very seriously. He didn't want to be known as the head of security who let a dangerous criminal get away with one of the most powerful weapons in the universe. How would that look on his résumé? Not very good!

Cosmo assigned his best security officer, *DEPUTY YON-ROGG*, to work with them. Yon-Rogg had lived on Knowhere for many years and knew everyone who made their home there. If someone was acting strangely, or something was out of place, Yon-Rogg would be able to spot it.

"We'll find your dirty SKRULL spy," said Yon-Rogg, who was a member of the alien race known as the **KREE**. The **KREE** didn't usually like the SKRULL very much, because there had been a long **KREE-**SKRULL War that left both sides angry and bitter.

As they set off to search for the spy, Cosmo warned Peter not to tell anyone about their

"Yes, but ever since I absorbed **ALIEN DNA**, I've only actually been half human," explained Captain Marvel. "That's something some people on Earth don't understand. When they find out I'm not fully human, they always look at me a little differently, and I don't always feel like I fit in."

Before she could finish, Yon-Rogg ran up to the pair of earthlings, interrupting the conversation.

STAR-LORD, CAPTAIN MARVEL, COME WITH ME! I THINK WE'VE FOUND SOMETHING!

CHAPTER

5

Star-Lord raced down the street after Yon-Rogg and Captain Marvel. Just as he was passing the Celestial Boot's front door, the other Guardians of the Galaxy stepped out.

"Oh, Quill, there you are," said Rocket. "Just in time, come on! The Cosmic Circus just landed on the station, and we're going to go see the robotic lion tamers."

"Wait. . . . Are they robotic lions that are being tamed, or are robotic tamers doing the taming?" asked Peter, confused.

"Both!" Drax shouted in delight. He was always up for a good robot sideshow act.

"I am Groot," Groot added.

"He's right," Rocket confirmed. "It is supposed to be awesome!"

"I'm more interested in the living tightrope walkers," remarked Gamora.

"Wait. . . . Are the tightrope walkers alive, or the tightrope itself?" Peter asked.

"Again, both!" Rocket shouted. "You've gotta come!"

Peter wanted to. A crazy alien circus with robot lions and living tightropes. . . . Yeah, that sounded like it would be just up his alley. Plus, some hang time with the Guardians was never a bad thing.

But no. . . the fate of Earth, and even the

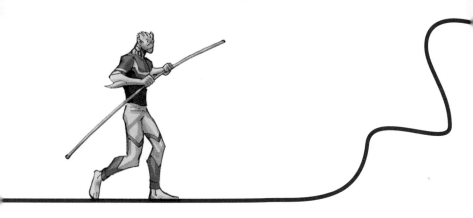

galaxy, was in the balance. He had to work now and play later.

"Sorry, guys. I want to, but I just can't," Peter said reluctantly.

"Why not?" Gamora asked. "What do you need to do that's so important?"

"I bet I know what it is," Rocket said. "Another human from Earth came to the station last night, and now you would rather hang out with her instead of us."

Gamora gasped. **"Peter, is that really what it is?"**

"No. . ." Peter started. He was about to explain the whole situation, about the Skrull and the missing parts for the Ultimate Nullifier, but then he remembered the warning from Cosmo not to tell anyone about his secret mission. This also went for his best friends.

"It is good to see another earthling, but that's not why I can't hang out right now. It's just that **I'm. . .not. . .feeling. . .very. . . good,**" Peter lied. "I've been, like, throwing up everywhere and stuff. Something I ate maybe? I'm going to head back to the ship and rest in bed."

Rocket eyeballed him. **"Well, you are looking a little feverish, I guess."**

"Okay," Gamora said. "You go lie down and feel better."

"I am Groot," Groot agreed.

"Thanks, guys. Sorry to miss it," Peter said, and he waved and wandered away. But as soon as he was **around the corner** and out of view, he raced in the direction that Yon-Rogg and Captain Marvel had gone.

Later, as Gamora, Drax, Rocket, and Groot stood in line to enter the Cosmic Circus Rocket tent, they could look down to see most of Knowhere. The Rocket tent was docked and hovering near the ceiling of the station, so anyone standing on the waiting platforms had a great view of the streets below.

"**I hope Peter feels better soon,**" Gamora said.

"**I am Groot,**" Groot remarked.

"What are you talking about, Groot?" Rocket asked his friend. "Quill's not down there. Didn't you hear him? He's back at the ship, trying to sleep off his cold."

But Groot insisted, pointing down to the streets of Knowhere below. Rocket, using his special **CYBERNETIC EYES**, zoomed in to see what Groot was trying to show them.

"Why that little. . ." he mumbled to himself. "Groot's right. That's Quill down there. He's standing at some warehouse. And sure enough, he's with Captain Marvel!"

Everyone was shocked! "But I thought he was supposed to be lying down in his ship," Drax remarked.

"Oh, he's lying all right," Rocket said. **"Lying to us, his so-called friends."**

"Oh, Peter. . ." Gamora murmured sadly.

CHAPTER 6

*A*fter leaving the Guardians at the Celestial Boot, Peter caught up with Yon-Rogg and Captain Marvel at a section of Knowhere that was mostly used for storage. All around them were old broken-down ships and pieces of large mining equipment that were smashed and rusting. The perfect place for a SKRULL agent to hide out, Peter thought.

The heroes finally came to a stop in front of an old warehouse that was practically falling down.

"Our security department intercepted chatter that some heavy-duty weapons were being smuggled through an **ILLEGAL TELEPORT NODE** set up in this warehouse," Yon-Rogg explained to the others. "Knowhere isn't a very large station, so there aren't that many illegal arms deals going down at any one time. The guy you're looking for *HAS* to be involved."

The three peered through the window.

"These two are **SHI'AR**," Peter said, naming the race of aliens he saw inside. "Not **SKRULLS**." **SKRULLS** looked completely different. They were green and kind of **LIZARD-LIKE**.

"Yes, but your **SKRULL** is a shape-shifter," Yon-Rogg reminded them. "He could be disguised as a **SHI'AR** for all we know."

"True," Captain Marvel admitted.

Peter and his companions watched at the window as the two **SHI'AR** pulled in several large crates. **"The weapons MUST be in those crates,"** Yon-Rogg remarked.

The **SHI'AR** turned a button on a teleporter device, and as soon as it came on, they began pushing crates through the portal that it created.

"This is happening right now!" Yon-Rogg

shouted. "They're already teleporting the weapons out!"

"MOVE IN!" Captain Marvel shouted.

But the **SHI'AR** didn't have any plans to be captured. They fired blasters of their own and

EVERYONE JUMPED INTO ACTION!

Captain Marvel flew at one of the **SHI'AR**, using her super powers to shoot bolts of energy from her fingertips. At the same time, Star-Lord and Yon-Rogg both attacked the other Shi'ar.

The first **SHI'AR** landed a blast on Captain Marvel that knocked her across the room, where she smashed into a pile of old equipment. Free of her attack, the **SHI'AR** pulled open one of the crates in front of him. The opened crate held a wide variety of exotic weapons, including some that looked like long tubes with little hoses on the end.

While the first **SHI'AR** pulled out the tube-weapons, the second **SHI'AR** kicked and punched at Yon-Rogg and Star-Lord with dangerously powerful blows!

"You're going to wish you just let us arrest you," said Star-Lord as he punched back at the second **SHI'AR**.

"I doubt that," said the first **SHI'AR** as he sprayed Star-Lord and Yon-Rogg with the tube-like weapon in his hand.

Star-Lord and Yon-Rogg were **splashed back** against the warehouse wall, where the fluid they were sprayed with

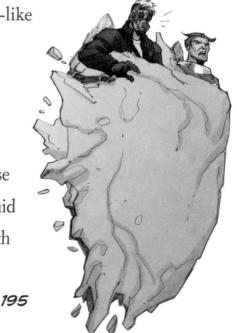

195

hardened instantly into an unbreakable foam! No matter how much the two struggled, they couldn't break free.

"And I have something good planned for your friend," the **SHI'AR** said. He watched as **Captain Marvel** pulled herself from the pile of twisted metal where she'd landed and prepared to launch a new attack. "This is a teleport grenade," the alien said.

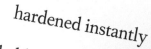

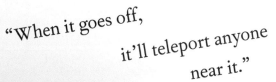

"When it goes off, it'll teleport anyone near it."

"Teleport them where?"

Peter asked desperately.

"Into the heart of a sun,"

the **SHI'AR** laughed.

"Say good-bye to your friend!"

He threw the teleport grenade right at Captain Marvel.

Oh, no!

Peter thought.

Captain Marvel's going to be destroyed!

CHAPTER 7

*P*eter watched in horror as the **SHI'AR** criminal threw his teleport grenade at Captain Marvel. And because he couldn't move, there was nothing he could do to save his fellow hero.

Or was there?

Peter's fingertips, the only little part of himself free from the foam, brushed across something in his pocket. It was one of the Space

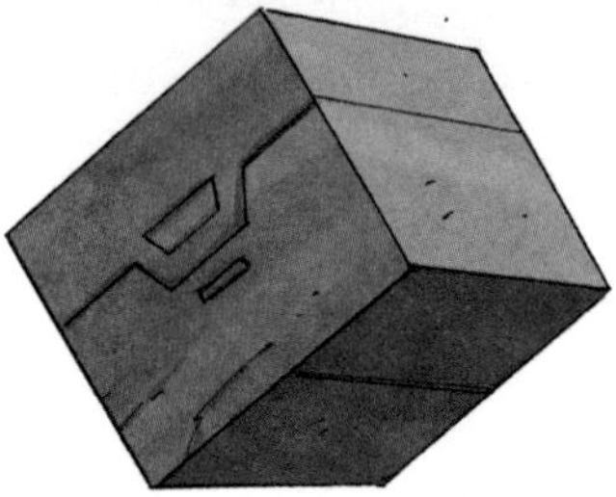

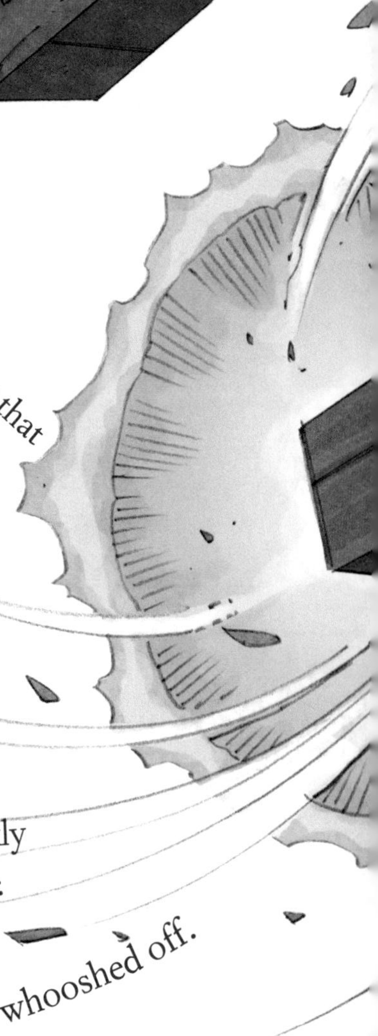

Darts that Rocket had invented—the ones that used homing beacons to go wherever you told them to go, even if you threw them in the wrong direction.

That was it!

I've only got one chance,

Peter thought.

Using only his fingers, he quickly worked the Space Dart out of his pocket and weakly tossed it out—but not before telling it:

"Teleport grenade!"

The dart *BEEPED* and whooshed off.

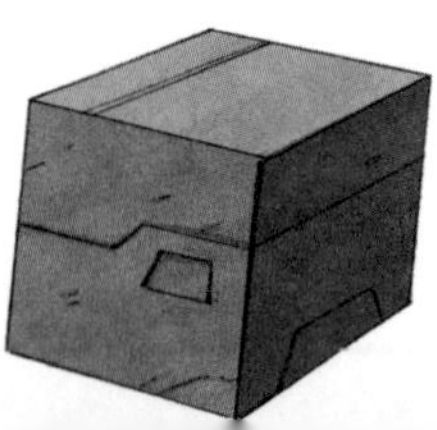

Even though Peter had tossed it in the wrong direction, and only with fingertip force, it still shot straight for the target.

The dart caught up with the teleport grenade, slammed into it, and set it off in midair, before it had a chance to reach **Captain Marvel!**

The grenade burst into a ball of teleport energy, but it wasn't close enough to Captain Marvel to teleport her away. Instead, it was close to the crates of **SHI'AR** weapons. It sucked them in and then instantly disappeared!

201

"Our weapons—NO!" the **SHI'AR** shouted as he realized that all the illegal cargo had just been whisked into the heart of a sun— and all by his own grenade.

But he didn't have much time to be upset, because within seconds Captain Marvel had rushed over and delivered a devastating punch, knocking him out. Captain Marvel then made short work of the second **SHI'AR** and used her energy blasts to free Peter and Yon-Rogg from the trapping foam.

"Thank you, Star-Lord," Captain Marvel said to Peter. **"You saved my life."**

"You returned the favor," Peter replied. "If you hadn't gotten the **SHI'AR**, I'd still be stuck to that wall, and who knows what they would have done to me. So, thanks."

"Now that we've saved each others' lives," Captain Marvel said, "I think you can go ahead and start calling me Carol."

"And you can call me Peter," he said, smiling.

Within minutes, Cosmo arrived with more officers from the security office, and the **SHI'ARS'** whole operation was cleaned up.

"So..." said Cosmo, "did you get what you were after?"

"I think so," Yon-Rogg said. "All of the weapons crates were teleported into the heart of a sun. If the parts of the Ultimate Nullifier were in those crates, then they were destroyed."

"Yes...*if* they were in there," said Captain Marvel. "But that's a big if. We didn't see inside most of the crates, so we can't know if the parts were in there or not."

"Plus, we were looking for one SKRULL agent," Peter reminded them, "but these are two SHI'AR agents. We've examined their unconscious bodies, and they definitely are real SHI'AR, not SKRULLS disguised as SHI'AR."

"Yes," admitted Yon-Rogg, "but like I said before, Knowhere isn't *that* big. The odds that two sets of illegal weapons were being smuggled through here on the same day must be very high. We can't know for sure, but chances are that the stuff we were looking for was in those crates."

"Yeah, maybe. . ." Captain Marvel said, deep in thought.

"But if the nullifier parts were in there, where's our SKRULL agent?" Peter asked. "And

why would he have given his cargo over to the
SHI'AR?"

"**A tough dilemma,**" Cosmo
admitted. "Maybe you completed your mission
. . . and maybe you didn't."

CHAPTER 8

*T*hat evening, after all the commotion of the day was over, Captain Marvel walked with Peter back to the ship.

"What are you going to do now?" Peter asked.

"I don't know," Captain Marvel said. "I know **YON-ROGG** thinks the pieces of the Ultimate Nullifier were destroyed, but how can I be sure? The fate of the earth might depend on this."

"By morning, we'll probably be able to question those **SHI'AR**," Peter pointed out. "If they don't know anything about a SKRULL agent, then we probably have to keep looking."

"Agreed," Carol said as they reached the front door of Peter's ship. "No matter what we do tomorrow, I'm beat for the night. Good night, Peter."

GOOD NIGHT, CAROL.

THANKS AGAIN FOR YOUR HELP TODAY. I CAN SEE WHY THE GUARDIANS VALUE YOU SO MUCH.

209

BZZZZZZZZZZZ ZZZZZZZZZZZ

Later, Peter was about to head to bed when there was a **BUZZ** at the ship's door. "Who is it?" Peter asked as he opened the door to find the rest of the Guardians in a group outside.

ZZZZZZZZZZZ

"Oh. . .Uh. . .I was just about to get some sleep," Peter stuttered as he moved aside, letting the other Guardians through. "It's been a long day."

"A long day of lying in bed?" Gamora asked. **"I hope you're not still feeling ill."**

Ill? What was she talking about?. . .Oh, yeah. . .Peter suddenly remembered his lie from earlier. He put his hand to his stomach as if it were hurting him. "I'm feeling a little better—"

"Stop there," Drax said. **"We know you lied about being sick."**

"I am Groot," Groot said, nodding.

"We saw you hanging out with Captain Marvel," Rocket reported.

"Oh," Peter said, surprised to be caught in his lie.

"If you didn't want to hang out with us, you could have just told us," Gamora said, clearly hurt by Peter's deception.

"No, I did want to hang out with you," Peter assured them. "It's just that something came up and I couldn't tell you what it was."

WE CAUGHT YOU!

"I am Groot?" Groot asked.

"Yeah," Rocket agreed. **"Why not?"**

"I promised that I wouldn't tell anyone what I was doing," Peter tried to explain, feeling **backed into a corner** at this point. "So I had to make up that story about being sick. Really, I would much rather have gone to the circus with you guys."

"Peter," Gamora said, frowning, **"you know you can tell us anything."**

"Yeah, what was so important that you had to lie about it?" Rocket asked.

But Peter was stuck. It wasn't clear if they'd actually found the Ultimate Nullifier pieces yet, and the escaped SKRULL agent was still out there some-where. In fact, it was even possible that one of the Guardians was kidnapped and trapped somewhere, and that one of the people in his ship right now was a SKRULL impostor. This whole mess wasn't over yet, so his promise to Cosmo still held. He couldn't tell his friends anything.

"I . . . I'd better not say," Peter replied. As he said it, he could see the hurt in his friends' eyes. They felt betrayed.

"I thought you were our friend, Peter Quill," Rocket said angrily. "I guess you never really know someone, do you? Come on, Guardians, let's get out of here."

The rest of the Guardians followed Rocket out the door, leaving Peter alone. He felt terrible about lying to his friends. If only he could explain! Surely they'd forgive him if they knew the circumstances.

But there was nothing he could do about that now, so he went ahead and climbed into bed to finally get some rest.

That night, inspiration struck Peter! The next morning, bright and early, he burst into Cosmo's office, where Captain Marvel and Yon-Rogg were already speaking with the canine security chief.

"Stop everything," Peter shouted. **"I know how to find the SKRULL agent!"**

"You do?" everyone asked as they jumped excitedly to their feet.

CHAPTER 9

"*T*ell us how to find him, Star-Lord!" Cosmo demanded as he, Yon-Rogg, and Captain Marvel anxiously looked on.

"It was something Rocket said to me last night," Peter explained. "He said, 'You never really know someone.' That means that even though you've spent time with someone, there might still be things you don't know about them."

"Yes. . .and?" Captain Marvel asked.

"Well, Captain Marvel is the one who told us there was a SKRULL, so it's obviously not her," Peter noted. "And when we first talked to Cosmo, we asked him questions that only he would know the answers to, so it's clearly not him—"

"Where is this going?" Yon-Rogg asked.

"It's going to you, Yon-Rogg," Peter said. "We never asked you any questions."

"I told you, he's one of my most trusted officers," Cosmo explained.

"Sure, you trust the real YON-ROGG," Star-Lord said, "but what if this is a SKRULL who has replaced your officer? What if the Yon-Rogg you know is prisoner somewhere, while this person lives his life?"

"Yon-Rogg isn't just my best officer, he's one of my best friends," Cosmo said. "Don't you think I'd know him?"

"**SKRULLS are good mimics,**" Peter pointed out. "Think about it. He's the one who is trying to convince us that the Ultimate Nullifier must have been in those **SHI'AR** crates that were destroyed."

HUH?

"THIS IS RIDICULOUS!!!"

shouted an outraged Yon-Rogg. "I think the Ultimate Nullifier pieces were in those crates because they probably were. Where else on the station would they be?"

"There's an easy way to solve this," Captain Marvel pointed out. "Cosmo, ask Yon-Rogg some questions that only he'd know the answers to."

"Okay. . .Ronny, what did you get me for my birthday last year?" Cosmo asked.

"What? You're buying this?" Yon-Rogg asked Cosmo, hurt. "You've known me for years."

"Of course not," the dog assured him. "Just tell me what you got me last year. We'll prove Star-Lord wrong and be done with it."

"I'm not sure I even remember what I got you," Yon-Rogg protested.

"Oh, no, you'll remember this," Cosmo said, encouraging him. "Just think about it."

Yon-Rogg was quiet for a moment, as all eyes were on him. Was he really just trying to remember something. . .or was it more than that? Finally, he said, "Well, Star-Lord is wrong. Because I'm not your average SKRULL."

I'M A SUPER

And in that moment Yon-Rogg transformed into a **GREEN-SKINNED ALIEN** with pointed ears and scales! The other three jumped out of their chairs with surprise.

"At least, I'm not *just* a Skrull," Yon-Rogg continued.

Peter had never fought a SUPER SKRULL before, but he knew that just as on Earth there were human Super Heroes with special powers, on the planet of the SKRULLS there were individuals with exceptional abilities!

Moving incredibly quickly, the SKRULL pounded Captain Marvel with a blast of PURE FIRE and knocked Cosmo away with a fist that turned into a giant hammer! Peter blasted the SUPER SKRULL, but before the lasers reached him, the alien Super Villain raised an invisible energy shield that deflected the shots. The SUPER SKRULL laughed. "Tricking you was fun. I'm sorry that it's over. But that's okay.

KILLING YOU WILL BE FUN, TOO!"

228

The **SUPER SKRULL**, still pinning Captain Marvel to the ground with fire, used his hammer-hand to SLAM Peter into the wall.

"I NEVER EXPECTED YOUR TINY BRAINS TO FIGURE IT OUT, EARTHLINGS."

"OFT!" The breath went out of Peter with the impact. He tried to get to his feet, but when he looked up, he saw that giant hammer raised and about to come down on him again—for what might be the last time.

Groot doughnut?

CHAPTER
10

Just as the Super Skrull's powerful hammer-fist was about to hit the already battered Peter, a giant wooden shield appeared above him! The shield took the heavy blow, protecting Peter.

Wait...that wasn't a shield. It was Groot!

"I am Groot," Groot shouted as splinters flew off his body!

The rest of the Guardians of the Galaxy then burst through the door to Cosmo's office.

"Hey, ugly!" Rocket said as he raised a hyper-blaster he'd just built. "I never thought I'd see a face as revolting as Drax's, but you take the cake!" He fired at the attacking alien.

The force of the blast knocked the **SUPER SKRULL** back, making him lose his aim. He couldn't focus his fire blast at **Captain Marvel** anymore. She was able to spring back up and shoot blasts from her fingertips at him!

"Rocket's right!" Drax shouted. He launched himself into the air at the Super Skrull. **"You are uglier than me!"**

As Drax swung his blades at one side of the Super Skrull, Gamora came up on the other side, chopping with her sword!

"You mess with Star-Lord and you mess with all the Guardians of the Galaxy!" Gamora shouted.

Peter watched all this with amazement. Even though he'd been so bad to his friends, avoiding them and lying to them, they still didn't hesitate to help him when he was in trouble.

Between the blows from Drax and Gamora and the blasts from Rocket and Captain Marvel, the Super Skrull was on the ground in seconds.

"Nighty-night," said Drax as he knocked the alien agent out.

Later, a quick search of Yon-Rogg's apartment turned up both the real Yon-Rogg, tied up in a closet, and also the pieces of the Ultimate Nullifier that Captain Marvel had come to Knowhere to find. With the Super Skrull now her prisoner, her mission was complete. **"The earth is now safe—thanks to you, Peter, and to the other Guardians,"**

Captain Marvel said.

"And thanks to you,"

Peter reminded her.

"I'm headed back now to return these pieces to S.H.I.E.L.D. and Nick Fury," Captain Marvel said.

Peter smiled at this offer.

Nearby, the other Guardians, who had heard everything, turned and walked away.

"Well, that's it," Rocket said to the others. "We won't see Quill again."

"What do you mean?" Gamora asked. "Even if he goes with her, he'll come back soon, I'm sure."

"No way," Rocket said. "Once he gets comfortable on Earth, he'll have no reason to come back here again."

"It's bad for us to lose him from the team," Drax said, "but maybe it's what's best for him. He has been unhappy here lately."

Later, watching from afar, the Guardians saw Captain Marvel's ship leave the space dock and head out of Knowhere through one of the

skull-shaped station's eyeholes.

"Good-bye, you stinking meat-bag," Rocket said, waving to the ship. All of the Guardians lowered their heads. They would miss their friend.

IT WAS GOOD KNOWING YOU, QUILL, EVEN THOUGH YOU SMELLED LIKE A HUMAN.

"HEY, WHY ARE YOU GUYS ACTING SO WEIRD?"

asked a voice behind them.

They turned. It was Peter!

"Quill, what are you doing here?" Drax asked.

"Yeah, we thought you were on that ship for Earth," Gamora said.

"What? Why would I be?" Peter asked.

"Because you were all home-sick and mopey and everything," Rocket pointed out.

"Well, true," Peter admitted, looking at them. "I'm sorry I lied to you. But even though I hadn't been treating you very well, you still were all willing to jump in and risk yourselves to rescue me." Peter gave them a significant look. **"And that...is what a family does."**

"But...but...Peter..." Gamora stammered. "Don't you want to go home?"

"You know what I've finally figured out, Gamora?" Peter asked. **"I'm already home."**

They all smiled at each other.

"All right, enough with this mushy stuff," Rocket said, pretending like he was too much of a tough guy to be moved by Peter's words. "With that settled, let's go to the Orlani races!"

"I am Groot!" Groot shouted excitedly.

That night, their favorite Orlani lost the race, but they didn't mind. They were together.

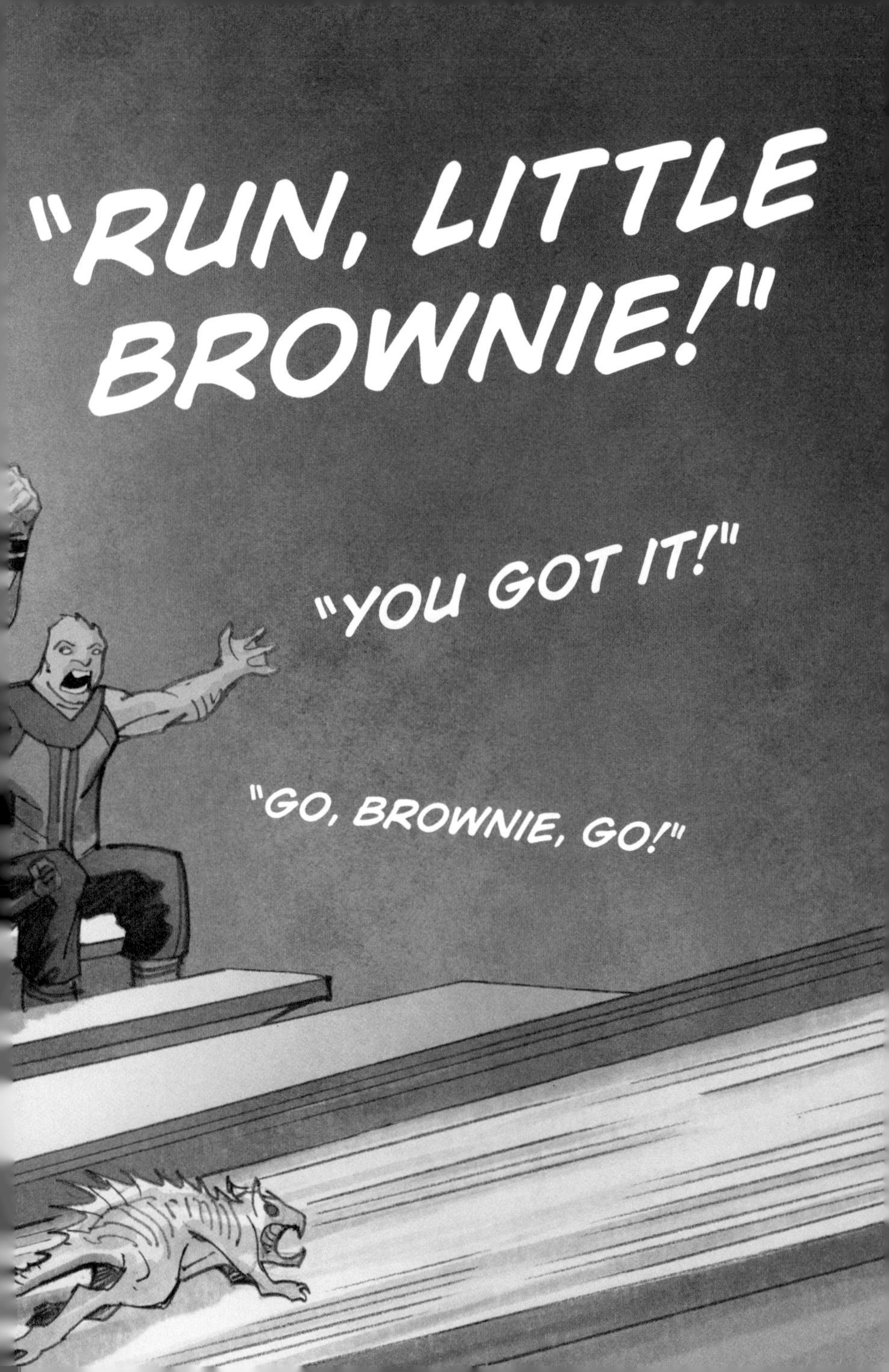
"RUN, LITTLE BROWNIE!"
"YOU GOT IT!"
"GO, BROWNIE, GO!"

LENT

STARRING

ANT-MAN

BY **CHRIS "DOC" WYATT**

ILLUSTRATED BY

KHOI PHAM AND **CHRIS SOTOMAYOR**

FEATURING YOUR FAVORITES!

ANT-MAN

EUCLID

CAPTAIN AMERICA

IRON MAN

HULK

BRUCE BANNER

HAWKEYE

BLACK WIDOW

FALCON

THOR

HELICARRIER

ROBOT

THE LIVING UNDEAD

ANT ZOMBIES

COUNT NEFARIA

ZOMBIE VIRUS

THE STORY OF ANT-MAN

*L*ife has never been easy for **Scott Lang**, an electronics expert who was forced into a career of crime to help his family. Scott always regretted breaking the law and only wanted to do what was right.

One day the famous scientist **Dr. Hank Pym** reached out to Scott and provided a way for him to put an end to his life of crime. Using gear invented by Dr. Pym, Scott became the astonishing Ant-Man, a hero capable of shrinking to the size of an ant, with the power of a hundred men.

Dr. Pym's technology revolves around the use of **"Pym Particles"**—an unusual set of subatomic particles capable of reducing the mass of any object. Scott, using the Pym Particles, has the ability to shrink not only himself, but also anyone or anything else. Pushing the Pym Particles, he can even sometimes enlarge things.

Pym Particles

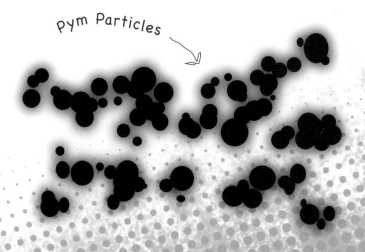

In addition, Scott can use other technology to communicate with ants and even summon them when they might be helpful. Since he's an electronics expert, Scott is continually modifying and expanding Dr. Pym's equipment, making it his own.

A dedicated hero, Scott Lang has put his past far behind him. Now he fights crime and protects the innocent as the astonishing

CHAPTER 1

It was a beautiful day in New York City, and Central Park was filled with the regular crowds. There were tourists strolling around, taking pictures. There were joggers steadily exercising their way down the sidewalks. There were picnickers, kids on school field trips, and artists painting landscapes. There were even a few celebrities, keeping their collars up and sunglasses on, hoping not to get noticed.

And yet almost none of the hundreds of people walking around the park even thought about the fact that there was a whole other world beneath their feet—the world of the

INSECTS!

Millions of insects made the dirt under Central Park their home, and on a nice warm day like that one, the bugs were even busier than the humans were!

There was, however, one person who was paying very close attention to the insects, and he didn't like what he saw.

"That's strange," said **Scott Lang**, the Astonishing Ant-Man, as he crouched to examine the tracks made by some ants that had recently passed through. "These aren't the traffic patterns I'd expect," he mumbled to himself.

Of course, it was easier for Ant-Man to notice what the insects were up to because of his amazing power. He did have the ability to **shrink to the *SIZE* of an ant**!

Right then he was no bigger than a bug, and he was standing in the tunnel entrance of an anthill.

"I need to find out what's happening," Scott said to himself as he followed the ant tracks deeper down the tunnel. To better understand ants, Ant-Man had been studying their behavior up close for years. He'd come to that particular anthill several times. And he could tell that something just wasn't right.

When he reached one of the anthill's main chambers, he was surprised to find most members of the ant colony lined up in a perfect row, standing at attention like little soldiers.

"What are you doing, guys?" Ant-Man asked out loud. Usually there was as much commotion in one of these chambers as in a New York subway station during rush hour, so it was eerie to see all the ants standing completely still. **"Are you sick or something?"**

Of course, ants didn't understand English, but Ant-Man did have the ability to communicate with them. Ant-Man's equipment could release **pheromone scents**. Ants, which had a much stronger sense of smell than humans did, used those kinds of odors to send messages to one another.

But even when Ant-Man released pheromones, the ants still didn't respond; they just stood there in a trance. They weren't asleep, but it wasn't like they were fully awake, either!

"I have to get to the bottom of this," said Ant-Man as he used a syringe to get a sample of an ant's **hemolymph**, the clear fluid ants had instead of blood.

Ant-Man stuck the sample in his handheld device, which clicked and beeped before flashing a report across its screen.

"A VIRUS?" said Ant-Man, reading from the device. "I've never seen this kind before, but according to these readings, I suspect it **could be passed to humans**!

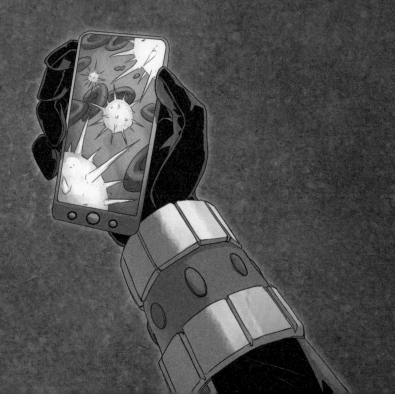

"This could be extremely serious," said Ant-Man, "like the time that space virus quickly ripped through a **S.H.I.E.L.D.** moon base. All one hundred and twenty agents were infected within hours!"

The space station incident had been different, because the station was contained, so the virus couldn't spread to Earth. Ant-Man didn't even want to think about what could happen if some unknown virus started to infect people across New York. It could quickly become an epidemic that could get millions sick . . . or worse!

Ant-Man knew immediately that he had to take his information to the best Super Hero team in the world. **"I have to find the Avengers,"** said Ant-Man. "I might be able to research a cure for this by myself, but if the virus starts to spread, it will take a whole team to manage containment. The Avengers will know what to do!"

Ant-Man rushed from the anthill. . .but as soon as he was gone, the ants he had been examining started to move.

Reaching the surface, Ant-Man sized himself up to his normal human height and rushed off to find Iron Man and the other Avengers.

As he left, he passed a couple picnicking on a blanket in the grass.

"Boy, the ants really are out today," said the man.

"Yeah, they're everywhere," agreed the woman. **"Ouch! I think one just bit me. . . ."**

CHAPTER 2

*I*t was easy for Ant-Man to find the Avengers. All he had to do was follow the sound of explosions and look for plumes of smoke. The heroes were clearly in the middle of a big battle.

"That way, Euclid!" Ant-Man shouted to the giant flying ant he was riding.

Not only did Ant-Man have the ability to shrink himself to the size of an ant; he also had the power to enlarge ants to human scale.

Whenever he needed to get across the city quickly, he used a pheromone scent to summon **Euclid**, his favorite ant friend, and hitch a ride.

"The Avengers are fighting the Maggia," Ant-Man said as Euclid landed on the wall of a building that looked down on the block where the entire Avengers team was engaged in combat with the criminals.

The Maggia, a criminal organization under the control of the evil Count Nefaria, had been caught red-handed breaking into a S.H.I.E.L.D. warehouse that held experimental weapons, but it looked like the fight was almost over. The Hulk was holding down four Maggia soldiers, Thor had knocked out several others, and an energy cage built by Falcon held most of the rest.

"Face it, Count," shouted Captain America to Nefaria, **"this little heist attempt has failed!"**

"The Maggia never give up!" yelled back Nefaria as he used a laser rifle to blow a hole through the warehouse wall and dash inside.

"Oh, no!" shouted Iron Man, who knew

what kind of weapons were stored in that warehouse. "Grab him before he can get the—"

BOOM!

It was too late! A giant robot, piloted by **Count Nefaria**, burst through the warehouse wall, firing a barrage of missiles at the Avengers!

THANKS TO THIS
S.H.I.E.L.D. ROBOTIC MECH-
ARMOR, NOTHING CAN
STOP ME NOW!

Seeing all this, Ant-Man knew he needed to help. "Get me down there, Euclid," he said, and Euclid took off toward the battle scene.

As **Nefaria's** missiles blasted Hawkeye and Cap, Hulk leapt to his feet. **"HULK SMASH!"** he shouted as he charged like a steam train at the giant robot.

"I don't think so!" shouted **Nefaria**, using the robot's claws to bat Hulk away. **Hulk went sailing through the air!**

Hawkeye shot explosive arrows, and **Thor** aimed bolts of lightning at the robot, but it still kept coming, knocking back **Cap** and **Black Widow!**

"How do we stop it?" Hawkeye shouted to Iron Man.

"I'm not sure," Iron Man replied. "It's based on my own designs, and I'm a pretty great designer! Maybe it doesn't have any weaknesses."

At that moment, **Nefaria** reached out with the robot's arms and plucked **Falcon** out of the sky, then slammed him to the ground!

The robot raised its giant foot, about to CRUSH HIM!

"No, say hello to Ant-Man!"

Ant-Man replied as he grew larger from out of nowhere. He was right behind the count, inside the robot's cockpit!

"What? Who?"

asked a confused **Nefaria** as Ant-Man's fist knocked him back into the robot's controls.

Falcon and the other Avengers peered through the robot's cockpit window, shocked to see Ant-Man inside. They had no idea that Ant-Man, shrunk down to a tiny size, had been able to slip into the robot's armor through an exhaust vent. Climbing along the robot's cables, he'd made his way into the cockpit, where he grew to normal size and attacked!

After knocking **Count Nefaria** out, Ant-Man shut the robot down and opened the cockpit. Then he threw the villain to the ground at the Avengers' feet.

"Thanks," said Falcon as Ant-Man climbed down from the robot.

"Good work, soldier," Cap said, patting Ant-Man on the back.

"So they do have a weakness," observed Iron Man as he examined the unpowered robot's exhaust vent. "I'll have to work on the design more."

"If your design was any better, I don't know if we would have survived," Black Widow told Iron Man.

Hawkeye walked up to Ant-Man. "Thanks for the assist and everything, bug-boy, but what are you doing here?"

"Right! I can't believe I forgot. **I have vital information!**" Ant-Man said urgently, taking out a high-tech device.

CHAPTER

3

"**Y**ou're showing us ant blood?" asked Hawkeye, confused.

"I'm showing you an image of the virus," replied Ant-Man, pointing to the scan on his handheld device.

"What did this. . .virus do to the ants?" asked Captain America.

"They weren't acting like themselves," replied Ant-Man. "They weren't moving around."

"Maybe they're just lazy ants," Hawkeye said, shrugging.

"No, it was like they were in a trance," replied Ant-Man. It didn't seem like the Avengers understood how dangerous the virus could be. "In tropical areas, there's a fungal infection that ants can get. This fungus turns them into **ZOMBIE ANTS**. My worry is that this virus might act like that fungus."

Hawkeye snorted. **"Zombie ants?"**

"It's real," protested Ant-Man. "Look it up."

"Can this virus spread to humans?" asked Falcon.

"It looks like it," Ant-Man responded.

Hawkeye sneered. "But you don't know for sure?"

Ant-Man shrugged. **"No."**

"This is all very interesting, but I'm going to have to cut it short," interrupted Iron Man. "I just got a call from Jarvis. A.I.M. is attacking in Battery Park. We have to get down there. . . . **AVENGERS, ASSEMBLE!**" he shouted.

The Avengers dashed off, leaving Ant-Man alone. Ant-Man knew that if A.I.M., an organization of evil geniuses, was up to no good, then the Avengers had to respond. But he'd thought they would help him with the virus problem, and they didn't even seem to believe him.

"It's like they weren't even listening," complained Ant-Man out loud.

Ant-Man turned to see a man in tattered clothes standing nearby. It took a second for Ant-Man to realize it was **Dr. Bruce Banner**, the world-renowned scientist.

Behind him, several **S.H.I.E.L.D.** agents were arriving to clean up the aftermath of the fight.

"Bruce, it's you. I thought you'd still be the. . .*other guy*," said Scott, referring to the **incredible Hulk**, whom Banner transformed into when he grew angry.

"Sometimes he calms down quickly after a battle, and then. . .I come back," explained Banner. "But tell me about this insect virus you discovered."

"I thought it was important, but the other Avengers didn't seem to think it was. . .so maybe it isn't," said Scott.

"Always trust your instincts, Scott," said Banner. "Even if others don't believe in you, you should believe in yourself. Especially if those instincts could save lives."

Scott nodded, understanding. He knew Banner was right. Working by himself, Scott sometimes felt unimportant, but Banner's words gave him a spark of confidence.

"So, what kind of virus is it?" asked Banner.

"Here, see for yourself," said Scott, handing Banner his device.

"Hmmm . . . You got samples?" asked Banner as he studied the data.

"Sure," said Scott. "Why?"

"There are a few more tests we should do," Banner replied. **"Come back to my lab."**

Banner's private lab was on board a **S.H.I.E.L.D.** floating fortress called the **Helicarrier**. Scott had never been on the giant airship and was excited to be there, but that excitement turned to concern as Banner showed him the new test results.

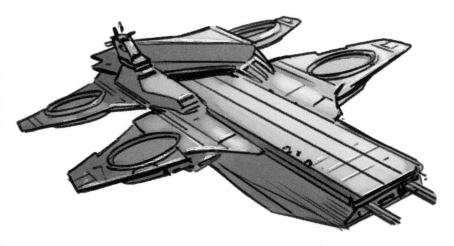

Banner wasn't an expert on disease, but he knew a lot about blood reactions because of his work in **gamma radiation**.

"Great, that's the last thing we need," said Banner, "a bunch of living undead making their way around Manhattan, like a *B-GRADE HORROR MOVIE*. . . . I need to let the others know how serious this is."

Banner called the communicator in Iron Man's helmet. Every Avenger had one of these **"comm units"** in or near one of their ears so they could easily coordinate with one another, even from different locations during battle.

"Little busy, Bruce," Iron Man responded over the sound of laser fire.

"I'm here with Ant-Man," Banner responded. "That virus of his? It's a **BIG** deal."

"Even if it is, we can't deal with it right now. We're under heavy fire!" Iron Man shouted. "These A.I.M. guys are acting strangely—more viciously than usual! And they just keep coming!"

"Iron Man, this disease could become a massive outbreak unless—" But Banner wasn't able to finish his thought, because he was interrupted by the sound of an explosion.

"Gonna have to call you back," said Iron Man as he cut communications.

Banner leveled a significant look at Scott.

"Well, for now, we're on our own," he said.

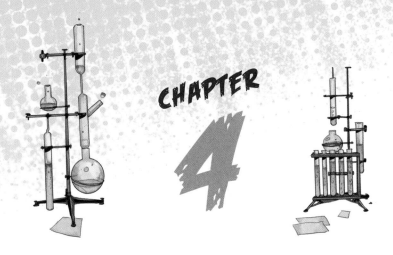

CHAPTER 4

"I've been with the Avengers for a while now," Banner shouted to Ant-Man over the rush of the wind. "In that time I've done a lot of strange things. I've fought alien creatures from space. I've visited other planets and helped defend a city of people who live under the ocean. . . . And yet I can honestly say this is one of the strangest things I've ever done."

Banner was saying this while clutching tightly to Euclid's back. When Ant-Man and Banner realized that the other Avengers weren't able to help, they decided to head back to Central Park to reexamine the infected ants, hoping there would be a way to develop a cure. All the **S.H.I.E.L.D.** shuttles were currently in use, so Ant-Man suggested they fly on the back of his ant friend.

"You get used to it," Ant-Man shouted. "Thank you for believing me when no one else did."

"Sure," said Banner. "I don't know why the others didn't pay enough attention."

"I do," Ant-Man replied. "It's me. I talk to bugs. I shrink. Those aren't really super powers. I mean, they are kind of, I guess. But Thor's a near-immortal Asgardian, Captain America's a living legend Super-Soldier, and Iron Man has more firepower than a small army. Hawkeye and Black Widow don't have powers, but they have years of super-spy experience with S.H.I.E.L.D. And what do I have? Bugs! If I were them, I don't think I'd take me very seriously, either. Let's face it, I'm no big strong hero like the Hulk."

"You think people look up to the Hulk?" Banner asked sharply. "When I become the Hulk, people only think of me as a monster. The Hulk is a hero and wants to help. But people don't understand that. They run from him, even when he's trying to save them. *Everything runs from the Hulk.*

"And it's not just when I'm Hulk—it's when I'm Bruce Banner, too," he continued. "Even when I'm human, some people still think of me as a monster. I went to a conference last month to present some of my research, but no one listened to my presentation. They spent the whole time worrying about making me angry."

Ant-Man knew what Banner meant. It was difficult being misjudged by people who hadn't gotten to know you yet.

"I started to correspond with some other electronics specialists I met online," Ant-Man said to Banner. "We traded ideas, brainstormed new inventions, that kind of thing. But when they found out I was a Super Hero, things got awkward. They stopped talking to me. I guess it was all just too strange for them."

Banner nodded, understanding, but their conversation was interrupted as Euclid came in for a landing. Ant-Man used his Pym Particle gun to shrink himself and Banner, but when they went into the same anthill Ant-Man had investigated a few hours earlier, all the ants were gone.

"That's really strange," Ant-Man said. "Usually there are at least some ants left to guard the tunnels. It's like this place has been completely abandoned."

When the two left the anthill and enlarged back to human size, Banner looked around. **"Hey, where is everybody?"**

Ant-Man saw what Banner meant. When he had been there earlier, the park had been busy, packed with hundreds of people. . . . Now there was no one.

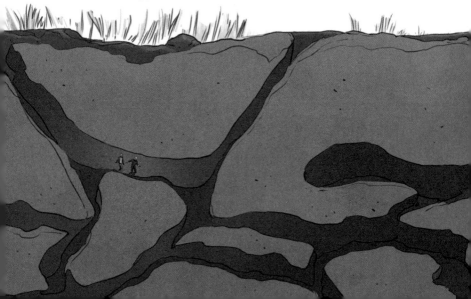

"Look at this,"

Ant-Man said to Banner, pointing at a picnic blanket that had been abandoned. "The sandwiches are half eaten, as if these people left right in the middle of their lunch."

"There are some people," Banner said, spotting across the park a crowd standing with their backs to the heroes. When Ant-Man and Banner got closer, the people turned on them and **SNARLED!**

Ant-Man was shocked!

Something was horribly wrong! Everyone in

the group had webs of pulsing blue veins bulging out all over their pale-green-tinted skin! Their eyes were a sickly mucus yellow and had no pupils!

"What happened to them?" asked Banner urgently.

"The undead virus! They've been infected!" shouted Ant-Man. **"They've become the—**

"LIVING UNDEAD!"

Suddenly, the whole group of undead jumped at the heroes, growling and snapping

their teeth! "This makes me miss hanging out with insects!" Ant-Man shouted as he dodged their bites.

CHAPTER

5

These "living undead" didn't move slowly, like zombies in old movies. Their arms and legs were stiff, but they could move very **fast!** In no time, the undead had Ant-Man and Banner backed up against a stand of trees.

"Don't let them bite you!" warned Ant-Man, trying to push the undead off him. "You'll get infected, too."

"**What can we do?**" asked Banner. "We don't want to hurt them. They're not bad guys, just sick humans. We have to help them!"

But as the undead roared and scratched at him, Banner felt himself getting angry. . . and starting to change.

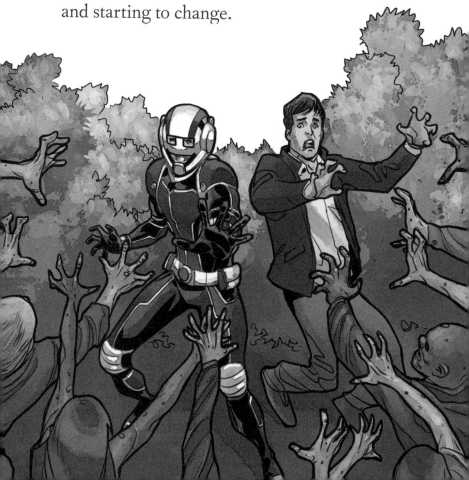

Ant-Man looked at his friend. Oh, no! If Banner changed into Hulk, Hulk might lash out against his attackers, hurting them—or much worse. Ant-Man had only seconds to figure out how to stop Banner from changing. . . .

That was when he spotted something on the ground he could use to solve the problem. To anyone else, this thing wouldn't have seemed like much, but because of Ant-Man's particular skills, it was exactly what was needed.

It was an earthworm.

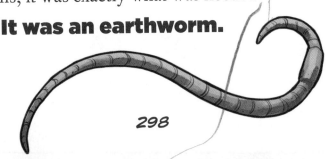

Ant-Man dodged the grabbing hands of the living undead and snatched up the worm.

Quickly, he tossed it between the undead and Banner, then **enlarged it!**

The earthworm was suddenly **huge,** and it became a living wall, with Ant-Man and Banner on one side and the living undead on the other!

299

"Are you okay, Bruce?" asked Ant-Man, putting an arm around the scientist.

"Yeah...yeah." Banner assured him, calming down. His transformation stopped. "But what do we do now?"

They could hear frustrated howls coming from the other side of the earthworm.

"I'll call Euclid," Ant-Man said as he released a pheromone scent. "We have something to show the other Avengers now."

"We do?" asked Banner.

Ant-Man pointed to his wrist, where a small wearable camera was mounted. "I got it all on video!"

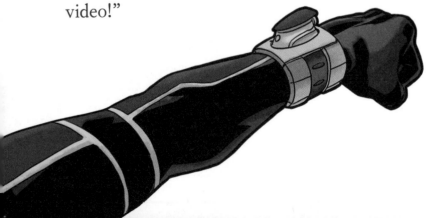

Back in Banner's lab aboard the **S.H.I.E.L.D.** Helicarrier, Scott uploaded the video files to the Avengers' server. Out in the field, the Avengers were able to use their hand-held devices to stream the footage of the living undead attacking Scott and Bruce.

"I'm sorry I didn't take this more seriously," said Iron Man grimly. He and the other Avengers were still in Battery Park, having finally just stopped the A.I.M. attack.

"How far has it spread?" asked Black Widow.

"We don't know exactly," Banner said to them over comms. "But **S.H.I.E.L.D.** is starting to get alarm calls from midtown. That seems to be the epicenter. We're in the lab now, because there's a chance that Scott and I can work up a cure."

"We've already got most of the materials we need," said Scott, "but the virus is spreading already. The Avengers can help by trying to find the infected civilians and quarantining them so they can't bite more people!"

"Look, you may have been the first person to find this virus," said Hawkeye, "but that doesn't mean you get to tell us what we should be doing—"

Captain America cut off Hawkeye's comment before the archer could even finish his thought.

"We understand," said Captain America directly to Scott. "We Avengers will head to Central Park and try to separate the living undead from people who haven't been infected. We want to stop the spread of this thing."

"It could already have gone farther than we think," said Iron Man seriously. "It might explain the behavior of these A.I.M. agents. We can't see their faces, because of the A.I.M. uniform masks. But they were fighting strangely, just like those living undead in Scott's video."

"If those A.I.M. guys are infected, then be

careful that you don't get infected, too," warned Scott. "It spreads through bites."

"We'll be fine," Hawkeye assured Ant-Man. "Like Iron Man said, the A.I.M. guys are wearing masks, so they can't bite us."

"Yes, but something must have bitten them to infect them in the first place," Scott pointed out.

"He's right. Everyone, check your skin and clothes. Make sure no ants have gotten on you," Warned Cap.

"Watch out!"

Falcon called, spotting an ant on Iron Man, but it slipped between two metal armor plates before Falcon could reach it.

"Don't worry, this isn't the first

time I've had a 'bug' in my systems," Iron Man joked as he quickly pulled off pieces of armor, trying to get to the ant. Despite what he was saying, Iron Man was clearly a little freaked out.

"Uh-oh," said Iron Man, suddenly stopping. **"I'm. . .I'm. . . feeling** STRANGE. . . ."

Then he dropped to the ground!

Falcon rushed to his side and scanned for the ant where Tony had removed part of his armor. **"Gotcha,"** said Falcon as he crushed the infected ant . . . but it was too late. The ant had already bitten **Iron Man!**

Iron Man's limbs grew stiff, and he started to moan.

"Tony? Tony? Can you still hear me?" asked Falcon. He got no response, but Iron Man started to aim his repulsors at the others.

"Scatter!"

Cap commanded as Iron Man fired at him and the others. All the Avengers dove for cover!

Horrified, Scott and Banner, on the Helicarrier, could only listen as the living undead Iron Man blasted at his teammates!

CHAPTER
6

Banner and Scott listened anxiously on comms to everything that was happening in Battery Park. Captain America, Black Widow, Hawkeye, Thor, and Falcon scattered, avoiding the repulsor blasts from the living undead Iron Man!

"We have to take Iron Man down without hurting him," shouted Cap as he raised his shield to deflect one of the blasts. "Even alone, an undead Iron Man could destroy half the city. We have to give Ant-Man and Bruce time to come up with a cure."

"My lightning will slow him down!" Thor said as he spun his war hammer, Mjolnir, in the air. Lightning shot from the hammer, slamming into Iron Man.

"No, Thor! Wait!" shouted Falcon...but it was too late!

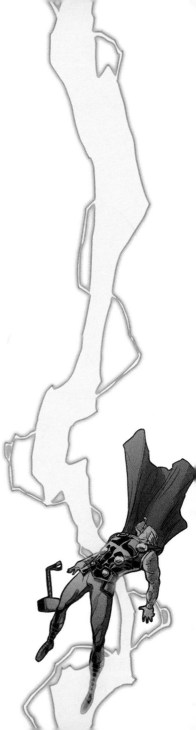

The lightning hit Iron Man, then blasted straight back out of him, pounding Thor to the ground!

Falcon quickly explained to the astonished Avengers, "Tony insulated the armor, designing it to be able to redirect lightning strikes!"

As Iron Man zapped the ground around the other Avengers, everyone ducked and rolled to safety.

"Did you see the raw power of that blast?" asked Widow. "It's like the lightning has supercharged Tony's armor!"

"Oh, great!" shouted Hawkeye. "With Thor down, what can we do?"

In his lab on the Helicarrier, a worried Banner looked urgently at Scott. **"We have to get down there and help!"**

"No, we can't help anyone until we find a cure to this ZOMBIE virus!" Scott replied.

"There's got to be something we can do," said Banner.

"There is," said Scott. "I can send a friend."

Only minutes later, undead Iron Man had Cap, Falcon, and Widow pinned down by fire when they heard Ant-Man's voice: "Sorry about this, Iron Man, but you'll thank me once you're back to your old self!"

Confused about the source of Ant-Man's voice, the heroes looked up just as an ant the size of a truck slammed into Iron Man, knocking him away!

"Now I've seen everything!" shouted Hawkeye.

But when the ant turned back to them, they could see a video screen strapped to its head. On-screen, Ant-Man explained:

LOOK, I'M STILL IN THE LAB WITH DR. BANNER, BUT WE SENT THIS GUY TO HELP.

It was Ant-Man's ant friend **Euclid**. Ant-Man had increased its size even more than usual and then strapped some gear to him, including the video screen. "I have a pheromone box attached to his harness," Ant-Man said. "I can send him scent messages remotely in order to communicate with him and control what he does."

Undead Iron Man swung back around, and Euclid wasted no time jumping into the fight with him. Iron Man's repulsor blasts bounced off the energy deflectors Ant-Man had built into the ant's harness. It charged at Iron Man.

"I never expected to find myself saying this," said Cap, **"but come on, everyone, let's give that ant some backup!"**

In the lab, Scott watched on the screen as Euclid and the Avengers battled undead Iron Man. Then he turned back to his work with Dr. Banner.

"This last batch might be the solution we need. Let's check," said Banner, using an eyedropper to put some chemicals on a slide, then examining the results under a microscope.

As Banner watched, the chemicals attacked the sample viruses on the microscope slide.

"It seems to be working," Banner said, but then added, **"Wait, wait. . . . No . . ."**

To Banner's disappointment, each of the sample viruses was able to repel the chemicals.

"It's as if the cure wants to work but has trouble bonding with the virus," complained a frustrated Banner.

"**Hmmm. . .**This all started with the ants in Central Park," Scott said. "Maybe the virus is more adapted to ant physiology. Let's try using ant hemolymph as the bonding agent!"

"**Brilliant,**" said Banner. Quickly the two men prepared another slide and stuck it under the microscope. Peering through the lens, Banner watched as the new version of the cure killed all the sample viruses on the slide.

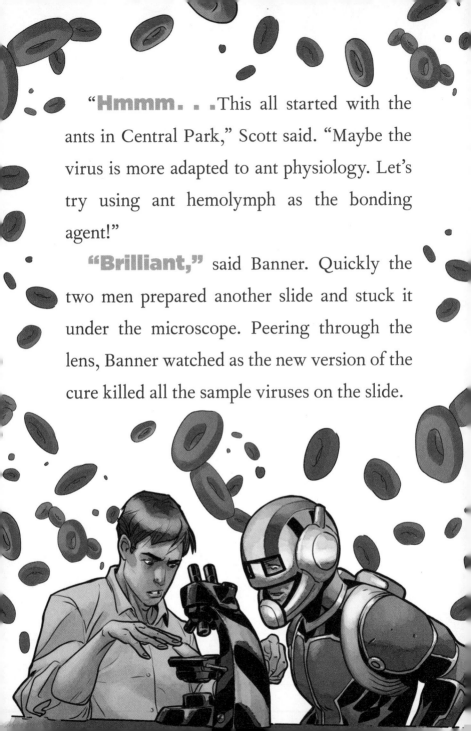

"We did it!" shouted Banner, excited.

"Well, it works in the lab, anyway," said Scott. **"But now we're going to need to test it on humans."**

"For that we'll need a test subject," Banner said. "We're going to have to catch one of the living undead and bring it back here."

"Oh, I got your test subject right here," said Hawkeye as he and Cap entered the lab, carrying an unconscious Tony Stark between them.

"With Euclid's help we were able to knock Iron Man out," said Cap. **"If there's a chance you can cure Tony, we need to take it."**

"All right," agreed Scott. "Let's get him up on the table, remove his armor and hope that we can turn him back to normal."

CHAPTER 7

"*A*re you sure we have to do this?" asked Banner.

Cap and Hawkeye watched as Banner and Scott prepped to test the cure on Tony Stark. The other Avengers were out in the streets, doing their best to protect bystanders from the growing crowds of infected people who were turning into the living undead.

"I'm sorry, Doctor, but we do,"

Scott replied. "If we're going to mass-produce the cure, we're going to need to take readings from the moment the chemicals first touch the virus. In this lab, we don't have instruments sensitive enough to get those readings from outside his body. With what we have available, the only way I know how to do it is to literally shrink someone down and send him in with the cure. So I'll use my Pym Particles to micro-size you, then inject you into Tony's bloodstream."

"Me?" asked Banner, surprised.

"Yes," confirmed Scott. "As you deliver the cure to the virus, you'll also operate a probe to take the readings. Remember: we need that data if we want to have any hope of helping New York!"

"You have to send someone else," insisted Banner. "Being inside Tony, curing him, getting the vital readings . . . that's a lot of pressure. If something pushes me over the edge, I could turn into the Hulk. . . ."

Scott nodded grimly. He knew exactly what could happen if a confused and angry Hulk rampaged through Tony Stark's bloodstream. Imagine having a tiny Hulk swim into your heart. . . not a pretty picture.

"Bruce is right. Send one of us," suggested Cap, referring to Hawkeye and himself.

"I wish I could," Scott said. "But you two don't know how to work the probe. Neither do I. I understand the electrical systems, but it requires specialized operation that I've just never trained for. Dr. Banner uses this probe all the time in his gamma research. It has to be him."

Cap, Banner, and Hawkeye all shared uncomfortable looks.

Scott sighed, then looked at Banner. "I understand why you're uncomfortable, but, Dr. Banner, earlier you told me I needed to believe in myself. Well, now it's your turn to do just that. You *can* do this. . . . You *have to.*"

Banner looked at Scott and knew he was right. He nodded. "Okay," the scientist said. "If we're really going to do this, let's move quickly. The undead virus must be spreading through the city like wildfire."

Working quickly, Banner got suited up in breathing gear, and Scott shrank him and a canister of the new cure down to microscopic size. Scott then injected Banner right into Tony Stark's arm.

Dr. Banner had been to a lot of strange places as an Avenger: an antimatter universe called the Negative Zone, a subatomic dimension called the Microverse, and a couple of different possible future Earths. He'd even ridden on a flying ant named Euclid with Scott! And he'd thought that was as weird as it got. . .Nope, Tony's bloodstream was definitely the weirdest place of all.

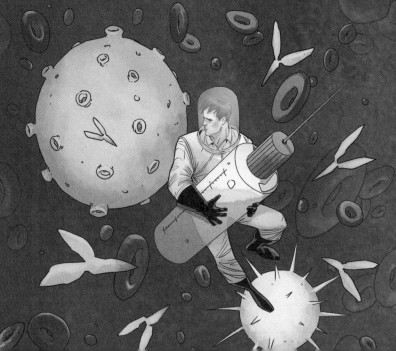

"Where am I headed?" Banner asked Scott via his comm.

"Just move forward—there should be copies of the virus all through his blood," Scott replied.

Suddenly, a small round white object slammed into Banner, knocking him back.

"What was that?" he asked.

"It must have been one of Tony's white blood cells," Scott said. "Tony's immune system thinks you're a disease."

"Not pleasant," said Dr. Banner. "I hope more aren't coming my way."

He looked up to see that, yes, more were coming—a lot more! Within seconds Banner was getting pelted by tons of white blood cells, as if a couple of teams of vicious dodgeball players were letting loose on him. He was being battered and beaten!

"You've got to help me!" Banner called to Scott.

Scott could hear by the tone of Banner's voice that he was getting angry: he was only moments away from turning into the Hulk!

"Dr. Banner, listen to me," said Scott calmly. "Once I was shrunk down and inside an empty beehive. I was surprised when the whole swarm suddenly came back. It was terrifying. Beestings hurt when you're normal size, but when you're tiny, they can easily kill you."

Ant-Man paused for a second. Was Banner listening?

"Bees can smell fear," Ant-Man continued. "And if that swarm had smelled my fear pheromones, they would have attacked me. If I wanted to stay alive, I had to stay calm enough not to give off the scent of fear in my sweat. By focusing on how I would feel once I was out, I was able to control my fear for hours, until the Pym Particles wore off and I went back to normal size."

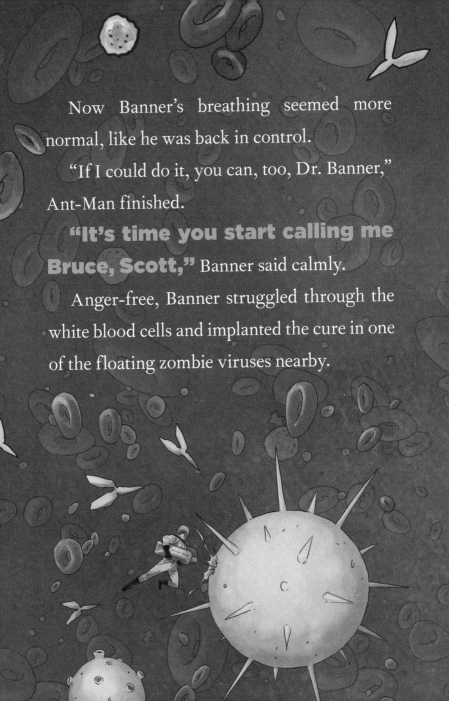

Now Banner's breathing seemed more normal, like he was back in control.

"If I could do it, you can, too, Dr. Banner," Ant-Man finished.

"It's time you start calling me Bruce, Scott," Banner said calmly.

Anger-free, Banner struggled through the white blood cells and implanted the cure in one of the floating zombie viruses nearby.

"You did it!" shouted Scott, capturing the data that rolled in. "We have what we need to mass-produce the cure!"

But then the lab door burst open, and in poured a team of **S.H.I.E.L.D.** agents . . . a team of infected, living undead **S.H.I.E.L.D.** agents!

CHAPTER 8

"*I*'ll take left, you take right!" Cap shouted to Hawkeye as he sprang forward.

Hawkeye instantly obeyed Cap's order, leaping into action by his side. The two were a blur of activity, knocking out one zombified **S.H.I.E.L.D.** agent after another!

But there were just too many of them! Living undead agents slipped past Cap and Hawkeye and instantly ran toward Ant-Man.

"I've still got to get Bruce out of there!" Ant-Man shouted to the others as he dodged the snapping jaws of the agents who came at him.

"Do it as quickly as you can, soldier!" Cap shouted back to him.

Between Ant-Man and Tony Stark's body, where Banner was still trapped, were three snarling and growling undead!

"Here goes nothing," Ant-Man said as he flung himself at the undead. In mid-air, he shrank. The shrinking moved him out of the way of some grasping zombie hands! Ant-Man quickly shrank or grew to different sizes as needed to dodge the arms of the agents who desperately snatched at him.

"*MOVE IT,* Ant-Man!" shouted Hawkeye as he knocked out two more of the agents. "We can't keep this up forever!"

Finally reaching the table where Tony Stark was lying, Ant-Man shrank down to about a foot and ran across the surface, grabbing the device needed to extract Banner.

"Hold on, Bruce!" shouted Ant-Man into his comm. "You're coming out, but we've got company."

Using the device, Ant-Man withdrew Banner from Tony's body, then hit him with Pym Particles. Banner grew to normal size next to Ant-Man. Ant-Man, too, returned to his usual height.

"That's what you mean by company?"
Banner asked, seeing the advancing
S.H.I.E.L.D. undead.

"Let's draw them away from Tony's
unconscious body!" Ant-Man said, grabbing
Bruce and pulling him toward the door, where
Cap and Hawkeye were trying to make a path
for them to get through.

At exactly that moment, Ant-Man's comms carried a message from Falcon. "Ant-Man, are you there?" Falcon asked.

"In the middle of something," Ant-Man answered, still pulling Banner through the room crowded with living undead.

"Fine—but we need that cure now!" Falcon replied. **"We just lost Black Widow to the undead team."**

Out in the street, Falcon and Thor were trying to push back a horde of living undead that was attempting to enter an apartment building filled with uninfected people. Euclid was still with them, bucking and knocking down rows of zombies, but there were too many of them.

"**The cure is developed!** We'll get it out to you as soon as we can!" Ant-Man promised Falcon. "But we have to get ourselves out of here first! It looks like the whole population of the Helicarrier has become infected!"

Ant-Man and Banner were now only a few feet away from Cap and Hawkeye, who had cleared a zombie-free path down the corridor to freedom.

"We're counting on you," Falcon called. **"Stay safe!"**

"We will!" shouted Banner, when suddenly a group of infected **S.H.I.E.L.D.** agents broke past Cap and slammed into Ant-Man

and Banner, knocking them to the ground.

"Or maybe we won't!" said Ant-Man as the living undead fell on them.

"**No!**" Banner screamed as one of the living undead bit him. "**They got me!**"

CHAPTER

9

Ant-Man pushed the living undead away from them, reaching out to Banner, who had just been bitten.

"I'm ... already starting ... to feel the change," Banner said as blue veins began to bulge out of his skin.

"Bruce, no!" cried Ant-Man as he kicked back more infected agents.

"It was great…working with you…Scott," said Banner.

"No, this can't be how it ends!" shouted Ant-Man.

"Oh, I don't think it will be," came a voice from the other side of the room.

Ant-Man and Banner looked past the crowd of zombies on top of them to see Tony Stark getting up from the lab table.

"The cure works!" shouted Ant-Man, a smile leaping to his face. "Iron Man's back with us!"

"Armor, to me!" Tony shouted.

Within seconds, pieces of the Iron Man suit flew through the door past Cap and Hawkeye.

"What a beautiful sight," said Hawkeye as the Iron Man helmet zoomed by.

Piece by piece, the armor slammed onto Tony Stark's body. In the blink of an eye, Tony had become the **incredible Iron Man!**

"These **S.H.I.E.L.D.** agents have terrible people skills," Iron Man joked. "Let's teach them some manners!"

BAM-BAM!

Iron Man blasted the living undead around Ant-Man and Banner. The zombies went flying, landing unconscious nearby. Ant-Man was no longer cornered!

He ran to the lab table and grabbed some of the cure that had just been tested on Iron Man. "This will do the job, Bruce," he said, injecting Banner.

"That was . . . as close as they come . . ." said Banner, his skin already turning back to normal.

Nearby, Iron Man blasted more of the **S.H.I.E.L.D.** agents.

"Don't worry," Iron Man called out. "I'm using the stun setting on these guys. They're good agents, and I want them to have a chance to get back to normal, just like I did."

"Thank you for saving us, Tony!" said a relieved Ant-Man.

"Well, the memories of my time as a member of the living undead aren't very clear," said Iron Man, "but I can tell that I must owe you and Bruce a favor or two, Ant-Man. And I had this crazy dream that a mini Hulk was in my bloodstream."

"Yeah...dream..." said Banner, his voice trailing off.

Iron Man looked confused for a second, then shrugged, saying, "Well, whatever you did, since I'm back to my handsome self, I take it you were able to create an effective **cure?**"

"We did," Ant-Man confirmed, "and thanks to data we received by testing it on you, we can turn the cure into a medical **mist**. It will turn the infected back to normal just by being sprayed on them."

"What do you need from me?" asked Iron Man.

"For now, if you could keep any more infected people from making it into the lab, that would be enough," explained Banner. "We just need time to make the mist."

"Consider it done!" said Iron Man as he zipped off to help Cap and Hawkeye fight.

Ant-Man and Banner immediately began programming the lab's medical equipment to produce as much of the cure in mist form as possible.

"Let's load the mist into canisters," Ant-Man suggested. "We'll create as much as we can before we run out of raw materials."

With Cap, Hawkeye, and Iron Man all working together, they had no problem keeping the infected **S.H.I.E.L.D.** agents out of the lab. It wasn't long before Ant-Man and Banner had created a stockpile of medical mist.

"That's all we can make for now," Ant-Man said, looking over the canisters. "Let's get this out to the streets and **hope it's enough**."

Soon Ant-Man and the other Avengers were spraying the medical mist on the crowds of living undead walking the streets of New York. The citizens started transforming back to normal within seconds, shaking their heads in confusion, as if they were waking from a dream.

"It's working!" said Falcon happily as he sprayed Black Widow, turning her back to normal.

Hawkeye had loaded the medical mist into his gas arrows and was firing them left and right into crowds of living undead. As the arrowheads popped, the gas sprayed out and cured whole groups.

Iron Man was flying over alleys packed with living undead, swooping in low and opening the canisters so that the mist spread over everyone. "I feel like I've turned into a crop duster," Iron Man joked.

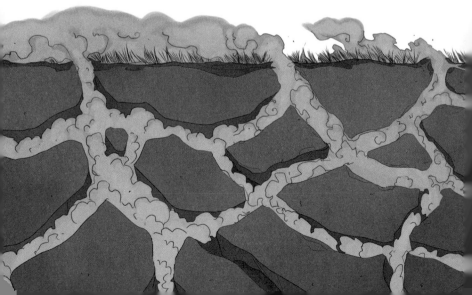

Thor threw a canister into Central Park, zapping it with a bolt of lightning and creating a mist shower. "There!" shouted Thor. "Now even Ant-Man's insect comrades-in-arms will be relieved of the sickness!"

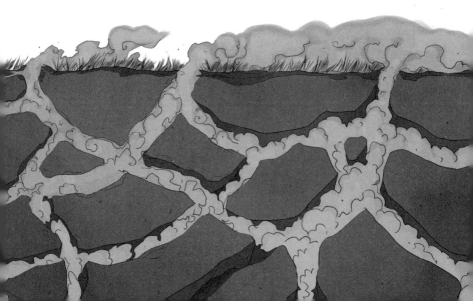

The plan was working, but Ant-Man and Banner checked out the remaining supply of mist, which was getting low.

"We can't run out of mist before we cure everyone," Ant-Man said. "If even one zombie is still out there, it'll infect more, and this will all start over again."

Banner nodded. "If only there was a way to get all of the remaining undead in one central place so that we could use the mist that's left to cure everyone at the same time."

"But how? What would draw them all together?" Ant-Man wondered out loud.

"They want to bite more people, so maybe we could use ourselves as bait," suggested Banner. "Get them to follow us somewhere that we can trap them."

"It's a good idea, but there are people all over the city that they could bite. Why would they be drawn to us?" Ant-Man replied. "We have to try something else. . . . If we can't draw them out . . . then maybe . . ."

Suddenly, Ant-Man remembered something Banner had told him earlier in the day . . . and it gave him an idea he thought just might work.

CHAPTER

10

"*A*re you sure about this?" asked a skeptical Banner when he heard Ant-Man's plan.

"Not entirely," admitted Ant-Man. "However, I can't think of anything else."

"But we've been trying to stop me from turning into the Hulk all day," Banner pointed out.

356

Ant-Man's idea was simple. "When we were talking earlier, and you were telling me how the Hulk is often misunderstood, you said, **'Everything runs from the Hulk,'**" Ant-Man explained. "I get why that's normally a problem, but now we can turn it into a strength."

Banner had to admit that Ant-Man was right: the living undead would attack everything that moved, trying to bite and pass on their infection. . .but if anything could get them to run, it would be a rampaging Hulk.

"Okay, but if the Hulk winds up busting up the city, I'm telling the mayor it was your fault," said Banner.

Banner nervously walked straight into a crowd of the living undead. It was easy for the scientist to let himself grow angry as the infected grabbed at him and tried to bite him. Moments later Banner's body started to grow and turn green.

His clothes ripped as his body mass doubled, then tripled, then quadrupled. By the time the transformation was complete, nothing recognizable was left of Banner. Instead, there was just . . . **the incredible Hulk!**

The Hulk roared, and all the living undead around him stopped advancing for a second. Even the sound of him was giving them pause. **"Hey, Hulk!"** shouted Ant-Man, shrinking and jumping onto his shoulder. "Can you hear me?"

Hulk looked at Ant-Man. "Little man Hulk's friend?" the green Goliath asked.

"Yes, but you see the zombie people? You have to chase them to this place." Ant-Man used a holo-projector to show Hulk a picture of

Madison Square Garden, an arena big enough to hold all the remaining living undead.

"Hulk just smash zombie people?" Hulk suggested with a roar.

"No, the zombie people are Hulk's friends, too," Ant-Man answered quickly. "They're just sick. Round them up, okay?"

"Okay," said Hulk. **"Hulk like chase!"**

And with that, he was off!

Ant-Man's plan worked like a charm. When the living undead saw Hulk coming, they ran as fast as their diseased zombie legs would carry them! It was just like Banner had said: everything ran from the Hulk.

"I was skeptical," said Iron Man to Ant-Man as he watched the Hulk chase the last of the remaining living undead into Madison Square Garden. **"But it looks like this is going to work."**

Black Widow and Thor helped load the remaining medical mist canisters into the building's ventilation

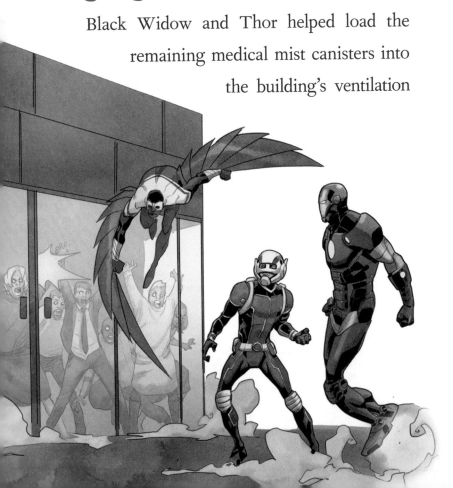

system, opening them before sealing the outside vents shut. They expected the ventilation fans to spread the mist through the arena, delivering the cure to all inside.

"You spoke too soon, Iron Man," said Falcon, scanning the building. **"It's not working. The mist isn't circulating!"**

Inside, Ant-Man could see that some of the living undead were already banging on the now closed Madison Square Garden entrance. A crack started to spread across one of the glass doors. It wouldn't hold for long.

"I'm on it," said Ant-Man. "Just tell me where the blockage is, Falcon!"

"I can do better than tell you," said Falcon as he projected a 3-D hologram from his handheld device. It featured a rotating image of the building's ventilation system, highlighting the problem spot in red.

Ant-Man studied the hologram for a second, looking at it with an eye for detail honed by hours spent poring over schematics of electrical systems.

"Got it. Wish me luck!" Ant-Man said as he shrank down to ant size and slipped into the arena's air ducts.

He scurried through the ducts, growing and shrinking as needed to fit through the different corridors and quickly making it to the jammed fan indicated by Falcon's hologram.

"Found it," he said, giving the fan a push to try to start it moving again.

But it didn't work.

"It's not moving," Ant-Man said, trying again.

"Maybe it's not a simple jam after all," suggested Falcon over his comm.

Ant-Man looked around and spotted the electrical wires that fed into the fan's motor. He popped off an access hatch and rooted around in the system.

"You're right, not a jam . . . we've got an electrical problem," Ant-Man announced. **"Good thing we've also got an electrical engineer!"**

Ant-Man patched together two wires. He instantly knew it had worked.

"Gotcha!" Ant-Man shouted as the air flowed past him.

As the mist circulated through the system and started to cure the remaining infected New Yorkers, Ant-Man jumped back out of the air vent and sized up. All the Avengers cheered and gathered around him.

"Tiny man now less tiny," observed a confused Hulk.

"I have to admit, you did great today," Hawkeye said to Ant-Man.

"And we owe you an apology," said Falcon. "If we had taken you more seriously right away, things would never have gotten this bad."

"That's not a mistake we'll make again," Cap stated.

"Definitely not," agreed Black Widow.

Ant-Man smiled. "Thanks, everybody," he said. "That means a lot coming from Earth's Mightiest Heroes!"

Later, after Hulk had calmed down and turned back into Banner, Ant-Man got a message to meet the doctor in his Helicarrier lab.

"Hey, Bruce, what's up?" asked Scott when he walked in.

"Nothing. I needed you here so you could get a **S.H.I.E.L.D.** security pass to our lab," said Banner.

Scott didn't think he'd heard that right. **"Our lab?"**

"Yep," said Banner. "You can't do all

your scientific work in an anthill, so I hope you'll join me here from time to time."

"Are you sure?" asked Scott. "I mean, I'm not sure the other Avengers would want me around. . . ."

"You're right," said Iron Man, entering the lab. "I usually don't like having competition in the genius department . . . but in your case, I'll make an exception."

"Genius?" asked Scott, surprised.

"What else would you call the guy who cured me, and half of New York, even after all the other so-called heroes had written him off?" asked Iron Man.

Ant-Man smiled from ear to ear.

"So what do you say?" asked Bruce. **"Lab partners?"**